Stories from the Heart

BY

STORYHEART

This book is a work of fiction. Places, events, and situations in this story are purely fictional. Any resemblance to actual persons, living or dead, is coincidental.

© 2003 by Storyheart. All rights reserved.

No part of this book may be reproduced, stored in a retrieval system, or transmitted by any means, electronic, mechanical, photocopying, recording, or otherwise, without written permission from the author.

ISBN: 1-4107-3647-4 (e-book)
ISBN: 1-4107-3648-2 (Paperback)

This book is printed on acid free paper.

1st Books - rev. 04/01/03

INTRODUCTION

This book consists of some of the love stories I have written over the years. Thousands have enjoyed reading them on the internet. I hope you too will enjoy reading them now they are in print.
These stories are short enough to read, over a cup of tea or coffee, or whenever you have some quiet time to yourself.
Yet long enough to bring a tear to your eye or a smile to your face.
All are written from the heart for you to enjoy.

This book is dedicated to those I love

Those I have loved.

And to all those hundreds of "friends without faces" on the internet that have read my stories and encouraged me to put them into print for others to read as well.

A special dedication goes to our special friend, Becky who sadly passed away February 2003. Without her help and encouragement through my darkest hours,
I would not have been able to find the
love and happiness that now fills my life.

INDEX

LOVE OF AN ANGEL	1
EMERALD EYES	5
WHY?	13
LOVE REVISITED	18
GHOST OF A DREAM	21
ONE AMONG MANY	26
IT'S NEVER TOO LATE	30
THE RADIO SHOW	33
SUMMER DREAMS	35
WHEN 3 BECOME 2	38
SALT WATER LOVE PART 1	40
SALT WATER LOVE PART 2	45
THE WINDOW	48
A ROSE BY ANY OTHER NAME	52
BATTLE SCARS	54
THE AIRPORT	58
THE KNIGHT AND HIS LADY	60
LONESOME DOVE	68
THE CHAMPION	72
THE OFFICE	79
BAR ROOM HEARTACHE	85
INJURED LOVE	87
ANGEL CAKE	88
THE 14th MAN	92
THE DREAM	96
HAND IN HAND	98
FOREVER	100
PURRRRFECT LOVE	103
THE PRECIOUS GIFT	106
THE GOODBYE	108
RIPPLES IN THE POND	111
THAT FATEFUL DAY	116
THE POOL	118
THE GREEN MIST	120
SIX THOUSAND MILES	124
THE RACE	128

LADY OF FASHION	133
ROMANCE	135
SILVER	138
MILLENIUM	142
CHRISTMAS STORY 1	145
CHRISTMAS STORY 2	149
CHRISTMAS STORY 3	152
CHRISTMAS STORY 4	156

LOVE OF AN ANGEL

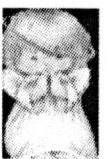

It had been a long couple of days, and sleep leaden eye lids felt like they were being propped open by matchsticks, as once more I started to try and scan the skies. I did not know what I was looking for; all I had was a memory, a beautiful memory, and the soft feel of a kiss that still tingled on my lips. Sleep was not far away, and with it would come the memory, the happiness and once again the pain. Then, the whole cycle would start again, the constant scanning of the skies and the searching for an Angel.

When had it started? Days, weeks maybe even months ago, I tried to think, it had been one fine spring day, letting out a little laugh, hell it had only been last month.

I had been walking through some small hills, I was on a spring vacation and enjoying the countryside, the weather, and just being with nature. The day was fine, the sun shone and I was at peace with the world.

Suddenly, as can only happen in England during the spring, the weather changed. Before I could gather myself and start heading back to the safety of the inn where I was staying, the hills were covered in mist.

I made my way slowly along the path, as I went further on, I found myself lost, totally utterly lost.

I came upon a small cave in the hillside where I decided to rest until the weather cleared, I was not bothered, I had food and water if it came to it. I settled down looking out into the mist, breaking off a piece of chocolate.

As I gazed into the mist and munched on another square of chocolate, the mist made the shapes of the rocks outside look like all kinds of monsters and demons. I laughed, why one almost looked like a person walking towards me. I looked again, it was not a trick of the mist, it was a person and they were heading straight for the cave where I now sat.

I stood and waved, the figure seeing me waved back and was soon in the cave with me. I helped them struggle out of their rucksack, they then turned and I was looking into a pair of the most beautiful blue eyes I had ever seen in my whole life. And as the person pulled down their scarf from around their face, these blue orbs were only out dazzled by the brilliant smile, which was aimed in my direction. She held out her hand, for it was obviously a she, even the layers she wore could not hide that fact.

"Hi" came a sweet singsong voice that sent a warm shiver through my body "I'm Amy, looks like we're here for a while"

I grinned, "Sure does. Would you like a piece of chocolate", sweet talking fool that I am I thought.

She smiled that smile again and took the proffered piece.

She sat down next to me and soon we were talking about the climbing, the weather and ourselves. I knew her name was Amy, and that she was a frequent climber of these hills. In fact, she said this was like a second home to her. When the mist came down her only thought had been to find her way to the cave.

The sky darkened and the weather showed no sign of clearing. Realizing we might be here for the night we took stock of our provisions. We both had water, and some food. Aside from the one blanket at the base of my rucksack, we had nothing else to keep us warm through the cold night. I hunted around the cave, using a small flash light I kept with me and found some dry wood, which we soon used to start a warming fire.

We chatted and before I knew it, I was telling Amy all about my life. She seemed to understand every thing I said. She did not make comments, just the odd word of agreement or knowing, but I knew she understood everything. I laughed "You're like a guardian Angel" I said "the way you understand these things". I looked up as she caught her breath and a look flashed across her face, temporarily removing the smile, but only for a second. Instead of saying anything, she moved closer and my arms went around her automatically as her body molded into mine.

We lay there and the fire slowly faded and died. It was cold but we had each other. As the night went on, hugs turned into kisses and what had began as two total strangers, turned into lovers. It seemed so natural and so right. As we lay together afterwards, soft kisses and tender words faded and soon led to sleep.

I don't know when it was or what woke me. The sun was just starting to fight its way through the mist and I felt so warm and so comfortable, like being covered by a feathered quilt. I moved to find Amy and the softness moved with me. My half sleeping eyes realized that indeed feathers, feathers that belonged to a set of wings, covered me. Two lips gently kissed mine and I saw a golden halo surrounding the face of my Amy. "Hush" she said "You're all right. I told you this was my second home, but now I must return to my first. You are safe and the mist is starting to clear"

She stood then an Angel, shining bright, and I just stood there unable to move. She moved and gently, softly kissed me on the lips. "That" she said "Is for being you". She kissed me again, a kiss so soft, and so full of love, my heart seemed almost to grow wings like my Amy's. "And that" she said "is so you won't forget me, as I will never forget you"

With that, the light around her grew brighter and slowly with a last look of pure love, she turned and started to walk away, moving up towards the lifting clouds. A last look and a faint voice that said,

"Never forget me and what we are. I will be with you always, just look for me, and I will be there"

Then she was gone.

The mist cleared and I was alone again, I could not move, didn't want to move, something had just happened to me, which I could not understand. I was still sitting there hours later just staring up into the clouds, when the mountain rescue people found me. They thought I was suffering from exposure or mountain sickness. How could tell them I was in love with an Angel?

So here I was, as I had been every waking moment I could spare, walking the hills and just gazing at the sky, dreaming of a pair of blue, blue eyes, and a smile that outshone the sun. I know she is there no matter where I am. And one day, we will be together again, my angel, and I.

EMERALD EYES

The floor of the airport seemed cold under his feet, as he swung his legs off the cramped bench he had been trying to sleep on. Trying was not really a good word, he had been thinking, His brain was going over and over the last 4 weeks, and how it had changed his life.

Two weeks ago, he had landed in Athens, ready for a holiday in the Greek islands. All of it had been so strange to him, the sites, the sounds, the smells, and the heat. But he was here, the saving, the flight, all had been worth while. A coach and a ferry ride had him transported to the Island of Spetzi. A small dot of rock set in the beautiful Mediterranean Sea. He had found the small taverna he was going to stay at, the room was small and plain but all he wanted. The people who owned the taverna were friendly, and spoke enough English for him to feel a welcome part of their family.

The first day he had spent settling into his room. Then the beach, the sea and the bar in that order, and after a filling meal and much time preparing himself he had left to tour the night spots on the small island.

He had found several bars with heavy music throbbing from them into the night, and had met several groups of people, all looking for the same musical release. He moved amongst the groups making friends and passing time on several dance floors. Liquid flowed into him as much as the heat and the dancing helped ease it back out. His ears were buzzing as he found himself near the harbor, and up ahead music came from a small building.

"The smile on your face let's me know that you need me. There's a truth in your eyes saying you'll never leave me, the touch of your hand says you'll catch me whenever I fall. You say it best when you say nothing at all"

The soft sound of Ronan Keating's hit record came through the open windows, making such a change to the heavy beat his ears had suffered the rest of the evening. He made his way to the entrance and looked in. The lighting was dimmed, shapes moved around the dance floor, couples lost in the music and themselves.

He did not know why, but he went in and ordered a Mataxa and coke at the bar. The record finished and the lights brightened and t99he DJ once more cranked up the beat and the volume.

He did not really notice this. His eyes were locked to a vision dressed in a short white dress, which hid nothing of the tanned shapely body that had just stopped dancing to the previous record. As the beat and the lights came up, the vision looked straight at him, and she flashed a smile that out lit all the flashing lights of the disco. Eyes green as emeralds flashed warmly at him, even out shining her white smile. He could not move, he wanted to look away, but he just stood there like a gormless fool. Eventually she let out a laugh that sent shivers of pleasure down his spine, and turned to a crowd of equally tanned men and woman sat at a corner table.

He recovered his senses and quickly swallowed his drink, ordering another as soon as he could attract the bartender. He was just fishing in an ice bucket of water for one or two left over bits of ice, when a touch on the arm, made him turn.

There she was, the white and brown angel, and he looked into emerald eyes that seemed to go to his very soul, she smiled, and he melted.

"Are you by yourself?" said a voice like the trickling of a mountain stream. The accent was from somewhere in the valleys. He smiled back seeing the look of pleasure heightened in her.

"That would be great" he replied, trying hard not to shout YES! YES! YES!.

"If you and your friends do not mind"

She smiled that smile and his heart flipped again. Then as she took his hand in hers, he felt a touch that sent electric shocks through his body and to kick start his heart.

She led him across the floor to the table where her friends sat chatting. She quickly said "My name's Grace, no, please no comments" a little laugh like Christmas bells filled him with desire "What's your name?"

He grinned, "My name's Phillip, but most folks call me Pip" he smiled, and felt her gently squeeze his hand as she motioned a seat next to where she had been sitting.

The evening went by all too fast, the group was great fun and it seemed that he was accepted without any problems. Records came and went, he danced, and he laughed. He held Grace's hand, where it seemed his belonged. Nobody seemed to mind, they accepted that Grace had chosen him.

At last as the night started to turn into morning, the song by Ronan was played. Couples moved to the floor and in what seemed the most natural of actions, he lifted her to her feet, and gently steered her towards the dance floor.

The music flowed as did their bodies, they seemed to melt into each other, the stars shone, the lights, and the other people seemed to disappear.

"The smile on your face let's me know that you need me. There's a truth in your eyes saying you'll never leave me, the touch of your hand says you'll catch me whenever I fall. You say it best when you say nothing at all".

She smiled, and nothing was said, nothing at all, and he knew this was special.

The music stopped, but they no longer needed it. They kept on dancing, not taking any notice of the music, the people, lost in their own world. At last they stopped, and slowly he bent towards her and gently kissed her. Her lips opened at the touch of his, and he felt the pressure of her tongue fighting to push into his mouth. Her kiss was demanding, her body pushed against him promising much, sending his head reeling, and his heart leaping in his chest.

The taste of her, the softness of her lips went on and on, tongues fought to taste each other, wrestling to give pleasure to each other.

At last they stopped, and looking around realized that nearly everybody had gone. She took his hand and with a "follow me" dragged him from the Taverna, and lead him in the dawning light to a pathway, that lead down to the deserted beach.

She stopped and kissed him, then with a "last one in the sea is a catfish" turned, and shedding her clothes as she went, headed for the sea, he just noticed the smallest patch of white as she disappeared into the waves. With a shrug, he shed his clothes and followed Grace into the sea. He started slowly swimming towards where he had last seen the lithe body in the water. His muscled body easily moved through the water. He was just looking for her, when a hand suddenly grabbed him, and an arm went round his neck, followed by two lips that took the breath from him. His body was not meant to hide his feelings, and it did not take long for something to come between then. She felt his embarrassment, and with the laugh that sent the chills once more down his spine, struck out for the shore.

She was there shrugging into her dress, which when wet seemed even more revealing. He tried to hide his naked embarrassment and quickly pulled on his clothes which being wet was no easy matter. Eventually he was ready and looked up to see her looking at him with a huge grin across her face. She skipped up to him, and kissed him lightly on the lips "Now you can take me home" she giggled.

They made their way back through the town until they came to a small apartment, she stopped him at the door, and gently kissed him, "Not tonight love, I want to rest", but another night smiled a mischievous smile.

Somehow he made his way back to the Taverna just as the first kiss of dawn broke through and kissed the blue Mediterranean. It was a perfect morning and he felt like he was floating, as the old Taverna owner gave him a knowing wink.

He climbed into his bed and was asleep before his head hit the pillow, with dreams of emerald green eyes.

Sunlight was streaming in through the windows, but something else woke him up. There was a feeling what was it, a laugh that made his heart skip sounded from behind him. Self-consciously he pulled the sheet back over his naked body.

"Hey you're spoiling the view."

Came the soft voice that meant so much to him in such a short time.

"It's ok, I know the people here and they let me in. Its lunch time and I thought you might be hungry. They do really good grilled sardines downstairs."

He pulled himself onto his elbow, the sunlight shone through the window surrounding Grace, for of course that's whom it was, with a golden glow. He felt a huge surge of mixed emotion running through him, and his body did not hide it. She looked but made no comment, as if sensing his discomfort, she threw a towel at him.

"Here, have a shower, to wake yourself up, and I'll meet you down in the bar"

He threw himself into a pair of shorts and fell down the stairs not quite sure, what was going on, and If he was still dreaming. But there she was sitting at a table talking with the old Taverna owner; her tinkling laugh sent his pulse beating. No, this was not a dream!

She saw him coming, and said something to the old man that made him grin, then turned and beckoned him to sit next to her. Reaching for his hand as he did so, and leaning across to kiss him as he sat down.

The old man arrived with a cup of some lemon liquid, which he placed in front of Pip. "Taste it" said the vision before him, that he was still a having trouble believing was there with him "nothing like lemon juice, made with lemons freshly picked and squeezed today".

Storyheart

He tasted the bittersweet liquid, and his teeth seemed to crawl back into his gums. She laughed... "NO! Add some honey and hot water to it, pointing out the jug and bowl, he had not noticed. He mixed the lemon with the honey and hot water and again tasted it. The liquid seemed to reach every part of his body, and suddenly he was alive.

"Good isn't it?" came the soft voice of the angel beside him

Yes he thought, but was not thinking about the lemon drink.

They spent the rest of the day learning about each other. Grace he found out was spending her summer months lazing round the island. She was due to start college on her return to Wales, but was making the most of her last couple of months before the hard work started. She took him all over the small islands, showing him things of beauty all the time, the gentle lilt of her voice and the sparkling tinkle of her laugh kept him floating in his own dream cloud. Yes she showed him many beautiful things, but all were put into the shade by this goddess that talked and laughed by his side.

She showed him a small bay on the other side of the island, hidden from the world. They stripped and bathed, then as the suns red lips kissed the sea, and the evening cooled the sand, they found each other. He was no virgin, and knew the way to make a woman happy, but with Grace he reached highs he never knew existed. The animal lusts and power of there loving made both of them gasp with the shear veracity of their coupling. They clung to each other sated for now, lost in each others eyes, then as the sun was replaced by the moons silver sheen; they made love once more.

This time slowly, giving themselves to each other totally. Words only lovers understand echoed across the empty beach and silent sea. They came together in and explosion of ecstasy that he never knew existed. They curled up together, when the sun started to rise to greet another dawn, they slowly walked back to his room, bodies sweetly aching from their night of love.

The rest of his holiday flew by all too quickly, their world was one, their bodies, their lives, their actions as one. All too soon, it was their last night they returned to their own small beach, swam, made love, made plans, and swore that they would be together again.

He kissed her and told her he loved her, she laughed that laugh and his heart exploded as she told him of course she loved him too. They lay then curled up on the sand, looking at the moon that shined in each other's eyes.

The next day she held him as he went to leave her. He had spent hours trying to get through to his work and had arranged that he could have another week's holiday. He kissed her and arranged to call her the next day.

All the way home he thought of her, as soon as he landed he took out his savings from the bank and booked another ticket back to Spetzi and his love.

As promised, phoned her, she was there waiting, and at the news of his return so soon he could hear the happiness in her voice, and swore she was crying. He called her every night after that.

Mere words were not enough to ease the pain until he could be with her. The day of his flight drew nearer, until on the night before he flew back to Grace. He called as normal, but nobody answered the phone.

When he had not found her waiting for him upon his arrival, he went to the Taverna, as he got there, the old owner and his wife, looked at him and broke down into a flood of tears and sobbed Greek.

It had all been so sudden, nobody knew just how, but she had gone swimming at their beach. She had been stung by a jellyfish, and by some fluke of nature her body had a bad reaction to this and she went into a spasm, losing her life in the waves where only a few weeks before they had been together.

His world ended that day, his heart broke, his mind ceased to function, and he lost himself in bottle after bottle, lost in another time sitting there for hours on their beach, lost in the past. The couple from the Taverna, and Grace's friends tried to help him, but he did not or could not respond.

Now here he was, at a cold and empty Greek airport, his world was over when it had only just begun. His heart might mend in time, but he knew he would never find a love like the one he had just lost.

A laugh that tinkled like a waterfall seemed to float on the air, he looked up, and his empty red eyes, seemed to light up for the briefest of moments, before once more his shoulders slumped. He curled up on the bench once more trying to sleep, to find the happiness that was there in his dreams.

Stories from the Heart

WHY?

The lights flashed across the water, making a reflected image of the colors, these images broken into rippling shards every so often by a passing boat. Only for the mirror image to magically reform a few seconds later as the ripples stopped. The soft buzz of the insects evening concerto filled the air, molding with the rhythmic sounds of man made music. A cooling breeze wafted away the heat of the day, helping the heat of the night.

He checked the mirror once more, and flashed a smile, yes he would do. He looked at the reflection in the mirror, just 20, and not bad he thought, blue eyes looked back at him with a mischievous sparkle in each. Yes he would do.

Picking up a bag with the many changes of shirts he would need for the night, he set off down the path towards the town. As he neared the buildings, the sound of music increased, and his steps soon found the matching rhythm. He was about to start work.

He had come to the small island during his year out before college and stayed. He laughed, that must have been over a year ago. Now he was almost one of the locals. He spent his time working in the bars, the discos anywhere he was wanted. He loved the life and ohhhh the girls!!!

The women on holiday! You could always tell the new ones apart from the others, like a fruit that ripens; going from soft pink to painful red, to the sun-tanned goddess they left as. He loved them, oh how he loved them, waiting until they were ripe before picking them. His heart had been hurt, he had fallen in love a few times, but each and every girl he had been with he always treated like a lady and he had never just used a girl for sex alone.

Storyheart

Tonight was just like any other he worked, he moved behind the bar, waving to the others as he placed his bag out the back of the bar. It was early yet and just a few people were there, but he knew that soon it would be a mass of heaving bodies. He checked that the bottles were in place and full, poured as many of the club specials as he could and left them on a shelf under the bar. It all saved time. The ice buckets for now were full but in the heat of the night they would soon turn to water. Dave the DJ was playing some old music that he liked to play, which soon would be replaced by the pulsating beat of the disco music. The first of the evening crowd drifted in, and the bell was sounded for the first time, as the first tip was thrown into the bucket. It had been his idea to sound the bell or sound the horn when a tip was given. He was sure it helped increase the customer's acceptance of giving a tip, and added to the fun.

The bar started to fill, and Dave started to rev up the music, as the first bodies moved onto the dance floor. He moved up and down the bar taking orders, while serving others. He had practiced and practiced and now could manage three or four orders at a time. The tip bell sounded again and again, with the odd klaxon being sounded as a large tip was given.

The room started to heave and he caught the eye of many of the women, making sure he had a smile for all of them. Some he knew, some he wanted to know. The air beat loud with the music, men and women came together, each movement a hint and promise of things to come. He went and changed into yet another tee shirt, resting for a moment and looking round the heaving room. A figure at a table in the far corner of the dance floor caught his eye. She was not beautiful, he did not know what it was, something was different, perhaps the fact that in the whole crowd of people she was the only person who did not smile back when he flashed a smile.

He went back to work, but at the back of his mind he could not forget the girl. He smiled at the people. He joked, and the orders were met, but his eyes kept straying to the lonely figure at the table. Many times he saw men going up to her and trying every trick in the book to get her to talk, to get with her, but nobody managed. Her table had an assortment of drinks on it, but she never tasted any of them.

She sat with unseeing eyes and nobody and nothing could penetrate her shell. He could feel the hurt and the despair from behind the bar and his heart ached at the sight of her.

The time passed quickly and though, he was slipped more than one invite to a promised heaven, tonight was different. As the music slowed and couples left to continue their seeking of joy and fulfillment in other locations. His shift was over, he would pick up his share of the tips tomorrow, but for now, he had other thoughts and plans.

He moved to her table, and as he drew close he could see the streaks of tears down her face, and he sensed so much despair, so much hurt, it was like a force field surrounding her. He moved a chair next to the table and sat down. She did not notice him, or so it seemed, and for once he did not know what to say. He sat there and his own feelings seemed to be impregnated by her sorrow. Thoughts of home, of loneliness and a wasted life filled his mind. He had more than enough money saved up, he was good at his job, and the tip money alone was more than enough to keep him very happy.

After an age she looked up at him and the sadness he saw in her eyes almost knocked him from his chair. He involuntarily gasped as the wave of sadness hit him. He moved his hand, and gently touched hers; it was stone cold, like her heart. At least she did not move it away.

As she looked up and in a voice choked with sadness and tears asked one word "WHY?"

Without thinking his arm went round her, she froze, and he stopped, but with a sob that tore his heart apart she rested her head on his shoulder.

Storyheart

He did not know how long they sat like that; his shoulder was wet from her tears. The night was fading, Dave had passed the music back to the cassette player behind the bar, and the tables were cleared away as the first kiss of dawn was in the skies. The last people were leaving and they looked at him and the girl and placed the key on the table in front of him, so he could lock up. The room drew quiet and soft sounds played adding to the moment, his arm was round her and she seemed a bit more at peace with the world.

As the sun moved into the sky and the warmth of the morning started to seep under the bar door, without saying a word, they moved out of the bar and slowly across the road to the beach. He looked at her as their feet left two lines of footprints on the sea swept sand. She would have been pretty except for the sadness that covered her like a shroud. Her eyes were ever changing but now so red and puffed from her crying that it was hard to see them. Her face was tanned, and he guessed she had been there for a while. Yes, he thought, her face was not beautiful, but a face of beauty, her body now with his arm round it was all that a female body should be.

They walked along together, not a word was said, and at the end she looked up into his eyes, and kissed his cheek. But the look and the one word she had spoken were still etched in his heart "WHY?"

For the first time he went back to his room alone. He could not get her out of his mind. The sun came up and for the first time for a while reached for the phone and called his parents back in England. Of course they were surprised and overjoyed to hear from him. Of course they were worried about him, and were pleased to hear from him, and his mother let out a silent sob when at the end of the call he half whispered words he would never have said before tonight. "I love you, Mum"

The next night he worked and half of him was looking for her, but she was not there and it made the evening very lonely despite all the people in the bar.

Stories from the Heart

Suddenly as the music started to slow, she was there at the same table and his heart lifted, as the faintest of smiles flitted across her face as their eyes met.

As soon as he could, he made his way to her table, and this time her hand sought his. They sat for a short time, until it was time for him to go back to work. But as he went to leave, he felt a small squeeze on his hand, just enough to know somebody was there and cared.

This time he thought as he carried on with his work, looking at her at every chance, it would be different, she would never have to feel the pain, never would she ever have to ask "WHY?"

He knew this time it was forever, and his life would never be the same again. His world was now and forever linked with hers.

LOVE REVISITED

He sat on the edge of the bed, music played drowning out what should have been either the scrape of pen on paper or the tap tap of two finger typing as the latest masterpiece made it's much longed for appearance. Should have been! Were the right words, as at that moment the lack of inspirational creation matched the emptiness of ideas he had in his head. Littered around the floor were screwed bits of paper each with a broken dream of grandeur started on them, none with a finished article.

As the music played his thoughts once more asked why?? Here he was in his forties, and alone, TV dinner in the freezer for later, and no future. He had lost everything, the law courts had seen to that. When his divorce went through and he had given up his job along with his marriage. He had seemed to wake from a coma and realize there was more to life than what had gone before. Hence here he was now alone and trying to become a creative writer, be it poems, stories, songs, adverts anything. He just wanted to create, that's if his current mental block ever broke.

His thoughts turned to the past as they had often done during the comatose days of the unloved marriage. Thoughts of loves from his youth. Wishes, turning into dreams, regrets and what ifs. The girl, who he should perhaps have treated better, what if he had not broken of his engagement, what if he had chosen the other girl of the two, what if, but ifs are dreams and dreams disappear in the morning light.

His mind remembered a girl from long ago, they had virtually grown up together, she was a best friend rather than a sister figure in his early days. Last time he had seen her was 20 years ago, he had gone home to find her visiting his parents, and taken her out for the evening. Though both were just happy to see each other again, both knew by the end of the evening that when they got back into the car there would be a something they had never done as young children. The kiss, when it came, had been one he could swear he still remembered after all this time, or was that a dream as well. He had thought to see her again, but times, miles and other interests meant that nothing further happened. Sure he had heard news about her via his family, and had been saddened by much of it, but he had never thought to contact her.

Well he was a creative writer wasn't he, or at least that is what he was meant to be, so be creative, and write to her, contact the family and find out the address. He got on the phone and found out the little girl called Sam he had once climbed trees with was now a Mrs. Samantha Jones.

The next day he wrote a letter, not too personal, just saying what had happened in his life and over the last year or so, how he was trying to pick up lost threads from his past, and how she was one of them. He ended with the fact that he hoped she was well and they could get back in contact again. The next day he posted the letter and waited to see if the dream could ever become a reality.

A few days later a pale yellow envelope was sitting there on the mat when he arrived back from another fruitless trip to a publisher. It was from Sam, she sounded so pleased he could swear he heard her laugh as he read her letter. She said how pleased she was to hear from him, and some information about what had happened in her life. But most of all at the top of the page was a phone number, without thinking he straightway telephoned her, his heart giving a little leap as she answered the phone.

The years rolled back as they chatted, they were the same young couple from all those years ago. Talking with her was so easy, and he found that he was able to tell her things he had kept bottled up inside of him for ages. From the things she said her life had not been a happy one, but the more they talked the more it was twenty plus years ago, and they were as close as if they had never lost contact at all. More letters followed the phone call, and eventually he plucked up his courage and asked her out.

Come the night of their meeting he was not worried, and knew that everything would be all right before she opened the door. And when she did, it was the same Sam, a little older, but the laughter was there in her eyes, the warmth in her smile, and he was 20 years old once again. Time did not matter as the evening turned into morning, and talking, led to lips touching and no words needed to be spoken after that.

When he left in the morning, time seemed to have run backwards, he felt like a 20 year old and full of the joys of first love. That night they had laid bare both their hearts and souls, already they knew more about each other than people who had been together for years. The words and the actions had come so easy, and the future now had a meaning, a target, a star was there pointing the way to all that he had dreamed of and longed for. He knew no matter what, they would be there for each other from then on.

The days went by in a dreamy haze, and every moment with Sam was so natural, so right, so as it should be. And as his heart grew with the love he once had lost, but all these years later had found again, so like a cork popping out of the champagne bottle they used to celebrate their engagement, his creative talent unblocked.

He wrote songs, he wrote poems, and on the day they got married came news of his first book being published. But of all these writings, his first song that he written on the day after their initial meeting became perhaps his most famous.

The simple words that said how good it was to make a dream come true.

"Me and Mrs. Jones, we got a thing going on"

GHOST OF A DREAM

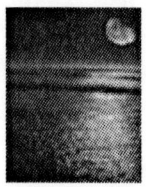

It was another day, the same as he had gone through many times before, from the waking, the routine of getting dressed, the same old drive to the office, the same people, the same banter, the same jokes, then the same drive home to the same lonely flat.

Let's face it, he said to himself, you're in a rut, and you have been for years, life was passing him by. He was happy in his own way, though now he had finally sorted out his messy divorce with his ex-wife he found himself sometimes feeling very lonely. This weekend he thought he would go down to the West Country, perhaps take a walk along some rocky pathway on the coast and stay in an old fishing village. He laughed sounded like an advert or the start of some slushy love story on a summer romance.

Still come the weekend, he was to be found driving down the motorway towards Devon and Cornwall, he had even booked a couple of days holiday for the start of next week, just in case. This caused a stir at the office for he never took a holiday. The music on the radio were songs from his youth, and his mind went back to happenings from his early days so that it came as a bit of a surprise to him to suddenly find himself in a narrow lane leading down to the sea shore.

He did not really know where he was, still he was there now, and it looked nice, so he stopped at the local pub, to have a well-earned drink and try and find himself some accommodation. He was on his second drink, the first not seeming to have touched the sides on its way down and chatting to the jolly red faced landlord, when he mentioned about a place to stay.

"Well" said Seth as he had come to know the landlord "Not many places this time of the year, I would say stay here, but I already have a guest, but if you don't mind I have a small attic that may do you?" He was not too bothered, he liked the old weather beaten Seth, and the weather beaten pub, and he was starting to feel a little sleepy after his trip down.

He soon decided to stay at the pub, and after sorting out the cost, went and got his bags before being shown his small but cozy room, where in a very short while he was fast asleep on the bed.

It seemed like only minutes later he was woken from a particularly interesting dream about a party he went to when he was 21, by what sounded like World War III coming from the landing below. He jumped out of bed, forgetting where he was, and the low beams, he thumped his head on one of the rafters. He groggily made his way to the door, peering down the stairs at what looked like a mountain of parcels with legs. He was just about to say something when the floor started coming up to meet him, hmm he thought just before his head and the floor met, I guess I hit me head a bit harder than I thought.

The first thing he remembered was looking into two of the loveliest deep blue eyes he'd ever seen in his life, surrounded by a blond hallo of corn ripe hair. The next thing was the pain above his eye and the feeling of hot liquid running down the side of his face.

"Are you OK?" a voice seemed to float down from a face that now seemed to like an angel looking down at him.

"Gee" the voice with the hint of a Scandinavian accent, "you've cut your head quite bad".

He put his hand up to his head trying to push himself up on his elbow at the same time and somehow hoping the room would stop spinning, his hand came away sticky with his own blood.

"I guess I must have clouted my head harder than I thought"

He tried to laugh but the effort made the room spin again. Instead he started to study the face of the administering angel that was now dabbing his head with a slightly dirty handkerchief, while helping him to his feet. It was the face of an angel, or rather a cherub, because the hint of laughter that seemed to play around the edges of the angels mouth were not angelic, neither was the look the blue eyes was giving him. Again he tried to get up, and that's when all the walls seemed to fall on his head.

The next think he knew he was lying in bed, but as his eyes focused he realized it was not his room or his bed. He put his hand up to his head and felt a bandage, but as he did so he also noticed that the arm was naked, as indeed when he looked under the sheets was he.

He heard a giggle behind him, and turned to look into the face of the angel he had met earlier. "When you collapsed that second time, you made me drop a bottle of red wine I was carrying" she giggled, "and being you, of course you had to fall right in it" He struggled to speak, but his head still felt like he was being hit by a hammer. She sensed his problem and put her finger to his lips, "Hey, rest you've had a nasty bump, and seeing as my room was nearer, I put you in here"

His head was reeling, strange things were happening to his body, feelings he long thought had been lost under the cover of a loveless marriage were starting to raise their heads. He tried to lift himself up on one arm and the room started to spin again.

"Hey now rest I said and rest you shall have" came the mock stern voice of his guardian angel, with that she leaned across and tucked him in, here scent filling is mind and sending his senses reeling. This was not helped by the soft kiss she left on his lips before, closing the curtains, and with a final

"Now get some rest."

She left the room. His senses and his now yearning body were alone again.

He awoke to the gentle touch of a pair of soft lips on his cheek, and for one instance thought he'd died and gone to heaven, "How you feeling today?" came the soft voice of the person, whose name he did not even know yet, but who twice now had made his body surge with want at the touch of her lips.

She gave him a steaming cup of tea and some hot buttered toast. He took the tea from her, again lost in her eyes as she smiled down at him. She sat on the edge of the bed watching him demolish the toast. "My name Sam" she said, "actually it's Samantha, but everyone calls me Sam" she smiled a smile that turned his heart inside out.

She told him about how she was studying the erosion along the coast line down by the harbor cliffs. He found he was able to talk to her like he had not been able to talk to any woman before. He told about his marriage, his life, his work and his dreams. Before they knew it, the sun was setting in the sky, and he had lost his heart. It had been so long time since he had known love. Then, with what seemed the most natural thing to do, as the sun went down, she took her clothes off and slipped into bed with him.

It had been a long, long time since he had given himself and had given to him, the love that they shared that night. They reached peaks that neither of them knew were possible, and he found a love that he had only dreamed about. Come the morning he woke with his body sweetly aching from the night of love, and his heart filled with longing for her, and the happiness of what he had at last found.

He reached for her but found only an empty, yet still warm pillow, on it was a note. "Morning my darling" the note read, "I will meet you on the cliff top if you fancy a morning stroll" he sniffed the note, smelling her scent and remembering the previous night.

Stories from the Heart

He slowly got dressed, still feeling a little light headed, not sure if it was from last nights happenings, the lack of food, or the bang of the head that still made his head spin. He made his way up the path to the cliff face, still clutching the note she had left him. His love saw him, flashed him the golden smile, and started running to meet him.

He was not sure what happened next, one moment she was running towards him a look of happiness and love on her face, the next, as if in slow motion she seemed to slip and start falling over the edge of

the cliff. With a cry of warning and anguish he rushed towards her. She slowly disappeared over the edge of the cliff, with what seemed to be a wave of good bye. He got to the edge and looked down, but there was no sign of her. His head swam and once again the earth closed over him as he sank to the ground.

His eyes opened slowly to once more look into the face of an angel, at first he thought it was that of his love, but then as his vision became clearer, he realized that this face was not quite the same.

"Are you OK?" came that same accent from this angel, "I could not bear to lose somebody else

here" she looked out to the sea, and carried on with a tear in her voice. "It was 6 months ago that my sister Sam slipped and fell from these cliffs.

I'm Sari by the way but most people call me Sue."

He looked into the same so blue eyes, so like his loves, and saw the sadness there, yet at the same time he knew that this was not the end, not just a summer romance. Sue helped him to his feet and they slowly walked hand in hand back towards the pub. Without noticing he dropped the piece of paper that had been clutched in his hand the soft wind sending it slowly spiraling towards the sea. He thought he heard a faint soft laugh that seemed to mix with the noise of the waves.

Storyheart

ONE AMONG MANY

From the start it had always seemed so right. Well the start was not quite the correct statement. It was the start of her breaking into the world, of her blossoming like a flower, from a girl to a woman. The start of learning to live, away from the security of her home and her family. Leaving the nest and standing on her own two feet.

She, like so many before, had learned about life and love, of self discovery and development in those precious years away at college.

It had been strange at first, without her family there. Making new friends, meeting people from different places and learning a different way of life. She had struggled a little at first, lost amongst all this new freedom. But, gradually she settled in, made new friends, enjoyed the fun, but never forgot the reason she was there.

Then, one day she met him. She thought of that first meeting and a smile crossed her face, her hand gently caressed the ring that now sparkled on her finger.

It was yet another party. The "normal crowd" was there, the normal "out of control people", the normal "talking in the kitchen crowd", the "dancing and hoping to meet the 'one' crowd", and the "well-it's-something-to-do crowd". Which crowd she was in, depended on how she felt that night. This night, she was just watching, not really looking for anything, just glad to get a break from her heavy weekend of revisions that lay waiting for her when she got back to her room. She felt a tap on her shoulder and turned with a smile to see a pair of the bluest eyes she had ever seen in her life. Her heart, for some reason, did a complete flip. All she could do was smile like some lunatic. A voice, which seemed to float from the clouds, asked her if she wanted to dance. She could not speak, so she just nodded her head.

He told her that he had been trying to ask her out for many weeks, how he had watched her at parties from afar, but was never quite able to pluck up the courage to actually speak to her before. That night however, it all changed, they danced and the music seemed to take them swirling amongst the stars. They matched, each smile, each move, each look, it was right, it was planned, the reason they had been put on this earth. They were meant for each other.

Days turned into weeks and they grew together, they became an item, a number, a couple. Everybody who knew them could see they were meant to be. Even her parents, whom she thought would never understand, and might pressure her about her work, seemed to understand. Her grades actually got better as they studied together and helped each other through that first college year.

At the end of that first year, she took him home with her, and her family fell under his spell, just as she had done. He became part of their lives, and her world was lit with their love. The next year, they did not even try to hide their love, but moved in together and after a small protest from her mother, even she understood. They were, in every body's eyes, as good as married.

There had been times, as with any relationship, when the seas of their love had hit a stormy passage, leaving both of them hurt and upset. Yet all the while they both knew that their being together was meant to be, it was right!

The second year flew by, this time she went back with him and met his family. She loved them and was accepted by them just as her family had taken to him. The third year and then the final year came and went, nerves frayed under the pressure of the final exams. They tried to be apart, to see if that would help the studying, but neither could live without the other.

Storyheart

The exams were taken and then came the day of the results. There were their names side by side both graduating with honors.

There families met at the graduation, and though they worried about this meeting, both families got on well with each other, their love seeming to cover all those who knew them.

They started work, and planned for their future. Again, she touched the ring that sparkled on her left hand. Remembering the day when he had asked her to marry him, she had thought she had died and gone to heaven.

The wedding was planned, and now here she was, on a plane, waiting for it to take off, so that she could become Mrs. Blair Westorn. She had said that name so many times, even practiced signing it, when she thought he was not looking.

The wedding was to be in her home town. He was traveling there with his family and would be on his way by now as well. She had sent her wedding dress on ahead of her, it would be there waiting at the local post office, along with her going away clothes, and a special picture to show her family.

She settled back in her seat touching the ring, thinking of the future and the life that would make her the happiest person alive

The voice of the pilot came on the intercom. "Welcome to American Airways flight 11 out of Boston, we hope that you enjoy your flight, and thank you for choosing to fly American Airlines"

She settled back for the flight as the plane took off. By this time tomorrow she thought, this time on the 12th of September she would be Mrs. Blair Westorn.

But, the plane never got there. She became just a name in a list of hundreds and then thousands.

A man sat waiting, watching the television, not believing it could happen. More than one person died that day and more than one heart got broken. His was smashed into thousands of tiny pieces.

Stories from the Heart

People turned up at a church the next day to view the joining of two people, but they left a few moments later, with tears streaming down their faces, as sobs of sheer pain filled the empty church.

A wedding dress sat unclaimed at a small village post office, until finally, a family member came to claim the package. It was only then, when they sorted through the items, that they found the photo. When they viewed the picture of her scan, they realized it was not just their daughter they had lost on that fateful day.

Storyheart

IT'S NEVER TOO LATE

He stopped on his morning walk along the sea front, to watch the children playing on the beach. Watching them splash amongst the waves, leaping in and out, the air filled with cries of laughter. His gaze swept along the beach taking in the families enjoying the summer sunshine. Some building sand castles or playing ball, while others were just lapping up the suns golden rays.

A ball came rolling towards him, and a "Hey mister, would you get our ball please" came from a small group of boys playing soccer on the beach. He knew what he wanted to do. He had done it so many, many times before. Just flick the ball up with his toe, onto his knee then volley it back to the waiting boys. His mind told his body what to do, but is no longer answered as it used to do. His attempt to flick the ball was slow, and he found himself scurrying around to pick the ball up and throw it back, rather than kick it. He was like a girl he thought, no not a girl an old man! "after all" he said to himself with a sigh, "that's what I am, an old man"

He moved to a bench and sat down, as if mocking him, the wind picked up the meager strands of hair he still had left on his head.

He watched the sun sparkling on the shimmering sea, and the soft gentle breeze sent his mind back, not that many years ago at all really, but it seemed a life time.

He had moved to the coast having finished his working days, and taken an early retirement. His life had been one of enjoyment, and now he needed a rest. Throughout his years he had known every emotion going from the happiness of love to the hurt of divorce. But now he had thought he needed a place to see out his last lonely years. Last, well at 50 it was not quite last, but lonely they certainly were.

He had found a small cottage with enough of a garden to keep him busy, a pub near enough to pass the odd evening, and views and walks to keep the body and mind in active.

He first met her on one of these walks, just as he had round a headland, there she was just sitting there gazing out to sea, the sun behind her, surrounding her like a golden halo. A vision which would stay with him, for the rest of his life.

It was the start of so many days and months of happiness, something he thought he would never experience again. After all, he was old, they were old, well she was not as old as he was. But is seemed she never saw that. She never once mentioned the years between them. And when once he had brought up about his age, she sealed his lips with a kiss and said "It's never too late to fall in love" the lines of an old song that even now echoed through his thoughts.

She soon moved into his little cottage, and their world was one of roses, sunny days and happiness.

A chill ran through him, like the first sign of the coming of winter on an autumn day.

The one night she told him she had been to the doctor, and what the doctor had found. He remembered the last few months of their lives together, and the bitter taste left by her death, a taste that poisoned his body and broken his heart.

Still photographs flashed across his minds eye, her smile, her serenity, and that first time he saw her, lit by the sun. Then the last time he saw her as he held her hand, as the last breaths of her life left her, and he could swear she was at that moment once more surrounded by that same golden glow.

A ball brushed against his legs, waking him from his daydreams. This time, he thought about it and kicked the ball straight back to the children, who waved and said thanks. He smiled and looked down at the last gift she had given him.

There in the pram he always pushed along the sea front on his daily walk, was the sleeping form of their child. He smiled, and the words she had said that one time came back to him.

"IT'S NEVER TOO LATE TO FALL IN LOVE"

It had not been too late for their love, nor for them to have their own daughter who smiled with her smile and kept her love alive forever in his mind and his heart.

Stories from the Heart

THE RADIO SHOW

She sat at her desk sorting through the pile of letters for the radio program, the "Lonely Heart Spot" letters. It was her job to sort through all the sad stories, some on paper spotted with tears, in order to try and find one for the radio station. She picked up a letter written on pale pink paper. "Dear Angie" it started as did all of them, for this was Angie's Radio Show, she read on.

"I would like for you to play me a record on your Lonely Heart Spot program for me.

Last year after 12 years of marriage, my husband suddenly left me for another woman. Devastation is the understatement as to how I felt at that time. I had not seen it coming, though thinking back, there had been signs, but like people say love is blind. So when he left me my world seemed to end.

I was lost, and had nothing in my life to live for, or to care for. That was until a friend introduced me to Geoff.

I was not really ready to go out, but Geoff was so kind and so patient that we went out, Geoff allowed me to literally cry on his shoulder, as I let go of all my anger and grief. He was so gentle, kind and understanding. After several months we started to go out, then just before Christmas we moved in together.

He understood, and gradually with his help and love, the pain eased and I found a new love with this wonderful man.

Then 2 months ago, Geoff, who was a trucker, was in a terrible accident, his truck was wrecked and he died."

The letters on the page were smudged at this point, but she read on.

"I wonder, could you please play me 'Show me the meaning of being lonely' for the love I found and lost."

She read the end of the letter and wiped a tear from her eye. That would be just right for the "Lonely Heart Spot" and the song was one of the most popular songs that Angie played.

She placed the letter on one side for the production. Then she slowly picked it up, and screwed it into a ball before dropping it in the rubbish bin.

How could she let the letter be used, she knew the hand writing so well, after all it was hers, and the ache would not go away no matter what song they played.

She hummed a few bars of the song, the letters would wait. She wiped her face; right now she needed tears, needed to ease the pain, needed something.

SUMMER DREAMS

The summer was never ending, day after day spent in fields of waving corn, the gentle sound of humming insects filled the air, and sensual concoctions of a an English summer meadow filled ones mind. In a giant oak tree seemingly there since the dawning of the ages, sat a young boy and girl, both touched by the suns golden paintbrush, neither caring what the world would bring, both lost in the joys of youth.

The boy stopped poking a stick into the tree trunk and looked into the eyes of freckled face girl who sat next to him, making a chain of daisies. His own pale blue eyes squinted as he looked into the sunlight which seemed to make a halo around the girls face.

"Julie" he said, still not sure enough of what to say or if he was right even trying to say it. The girl looked up and seemed to sense this was a special moment she smiled a smile that dimmed the sunlight on the summer's day. He looked and knew he was right, and it was right, this was the moment.

"Julie" he said, this time his voice was sure and clear, "We are good friends aren't we?"

She smiled again" Alex, we are special friends"

"Well" Alex continued "I know we are both young, and there is the rest of our lives ahead of us" he looked into her dark brown eyes, would she laugh? Was she laughing inside at his stumbling attempts even now. The eyes that looked back showed nothing but concentration at what he was saying, though deep down he thought he could see something else, something he was not sure of.

Storyheart

He stumbled on, "We have been friends for a long time, and well, I... hmmmm could we hmmmm I mean when we get older?" He was lost, he couldn't find the words.

She sensed his problem, and taking the daisy chain, placed it around his neck, then taking his hands in hers, she gently kissed him on the lips.

"Yes" she said "If you will wait, so will I, and yes, I feel the same" then slowly she kissed him again, this time with a kiss that went on like the long days of summer.

He was shaken, shocked, ecstatic, relieved, and so happy, all of these things and more. As the kiss went on he vowed to himself that this is what he wanted to fill his life, the happiness he felt now, and the girl he was with to be with him forever.

The rest of the summer seemed to fly by, everyday was an adventure in life, enjoyed together, and shared as one. The secret world of their love, that only they knew, whispered words amidst laughter, slow walks with tightly held hands, lost in the summer of their youth.

All too soon it was the end of the holidays, and they must part for now, tears had been shed away from other prying eyes, wiped away by kisses of tender young love. Now as the day of separation came each brought a gift for the other to bind what had gone before. He had given her a carved piece of wood, it had taken him hours and many attempts to finally get there initials joined together. She had given him a handkerchief, embroidered by her own hand "Alex and Julie Forever as One".

He had taken that handkerchief with him wherever he went from that day on until, as time went by; it lay forgotten at the back of the draw in his childhood bedroom. Forgotten that is for 15 years until he had discovered it again, and all those dreams of youth had come flooding back.

He stood there holding it in his hand, looking at the now fading letters picked out in ragged stitches "Alex and Julie Forever as One"

Where had those days gone? Lost in past.

"Alex" a voice came from outside the room "Where are you?"

It was his wife who had come to look for him, "I'm in here darling"

She came in, and seeing him holding the old handkerchief in his hand, broke into a huge sun bright smile that seemed to light up her brown eyes.

"Is that what I think it is?" she asked putting her arms around his neck

"Yes Julie" he said gently kissing her "Some dreams really do come true".

Storyheart

WHEN 3 BECOME 2

Autumn leaves crunched under our feet, like parchment. We strode on neither of us taking any notice at the trail left behind us. We had passed this way many times before, normally the air filled with joy and laughter. The sun always had shone, or so it seemed and they had always been happy times. We had looked forward to our walks, and we knew every tree, every bush, every nook and cranny along this well trodden path.

But this time it was different the very air seemed to cling to us, the dampness seemed to weigh heavy on our shoulders, and the piles of multi-colored leaves were like snowfall dragging at our footsteps. The birds which normally joined our joyful walks were silent, seemed to sense the depression and unhappiness that covered us.

This time it was different, this time something was not quite the same. I looked up gazing with my big brown eyes at the person I had come to love, walking by my side. His face was set; he seemed not to notice the surroundings or me. His eyes normally full of laughter now looked tired and red rimmed.

I tried to think over the last few days and what had happened, how our happy life had changed to this somber depressing state.

We had been three then, each in love with the other the world had been such a happy place, our lives content. I don't know what happened, but one morning when I went to join him in bed, he was not asleep as normal. He sat in the bed, hair disheveled strange water was coming from his eyes, something I had never seen before. He cuddled me into his arms, and I tried to kiss him letting him know I was there. Instead, he let out a noise that seemed to come from somewhere deep inside of him, a sobbing sort of cry an animal might make when in pain.

He buried his head against mine and again the strange water came from his eyes, I attempted to help but did not know what to do.

The next couple of days I just did not understand, she never came see us, and all he did was sit and stare out the window, or flick his way through pictures of our time together. I went out, I had to, I could not bare to see him like this, it was tearing my heart apart, I loved this man.

Then yesterday was it so short a time ago, I had gone to his bed as normal, to find him already up and dressed in a suit which I had not seen before. It was black, as was the tie he was attempting to knot. He gave me a gentle cuddle, and looked at me with those now red rimmed eyes.

That was the last I saw of him all day, until he came home late at night. I rushed to meet him, and he gave me a look of such sadness that it caused my heart to break. We sat on his bed, and he tried to explain that she was not going to be with us any more, something about a car, and a lorry, something I did not understand. We sat up all night and that strange water would often come to his eyes as he talked to me about her, and about how he loved her, as I did.

Now here we were walking as two where three had previously filled the woods with laughter. I was still here and loved him, as I know he loved me, but nothing could replace the love he had for her.

Once again I gazed up into his eyes, after all I was just a dog, and he was my master. And although I loved my mistress, I could never have loved her as much as he had loved his wife.

Storyheart

SALT WATER LOVE PART 1

It was a spring day, a gentle breeze, was enough to set the little wavelets skimming across the harbor, like so many small ladies flashing their white petticoats to the blueness of the sea.

He shifted his mind back to the task in hand, the boat would never get made ready by itself. He shifted the buoyancy bags, checked the ropes and pulleys, then the fuel and water tanks. All looked ready. He had already planned his course and passed it to the harbormaster.

This adventure had been planned for some time, to take the boat around the coast and up the River Avon. He gave one last look at the gently dancing waves, cast off, and ran up the sail.

After a while, once he was clear of the harbor, the fresh breeze sent him skimming along the wave tops. This was the life. just you and nature. He lost all track of time until his stomach told him it was time to eat, putting the boat on auto pilot; he went below and made himself some door-step sandwiches

He was just making his way on deck again, when his eyes caught sight of a small craft over on the port bow. It looked as if it was in distress, and as he turned towards it, a slim arm waved from the aft deck house. He moved along side, and could just make out the face of a woman, who seemed to be propped up against the tiller. Seeing trouble, he quickly tied the boats together, and leapt onto to the smaller sailing vessel.

A smile mixed with a grimace of pain met him.

"Am I glad to see you" said a voice that set his pulse running.

"Bloody tankers, no lookout, no lights, nothing just straight on, and the wash hit me, and.. Well.. "

She pointed to her ankle, which seemed to be twice the size of the other one. Luckily, he had some grasp of first aid, and soon realized that the ankle was broken. Going back to his own boat, he went to the first aid box and took out some painkillers.

"Here" he said "take these, they will help"

She sucked the tablets down, and soon, the look of pain eased from her face.

He did not know how long she had been like this, but it must have been some time, as she was soon either asleep or had passed out. He quickly and carefully lifted her, into his strong arms, and took her carefully over to his own boat.

He gently laid her in the bunk, making sure she was safe, and noticing the loveliness of her face, and the soft smile that played round her lips.

He then went back and tied her boat astern of his, making sure it was set for towing, last thing he wanted was a whale dragging behind him. Once done and back on board his own boat, he got them underway, and then went below, to check on his charge.

She was zonked, soundo, the tablets seemed to have done their job.

Gently he undid her jeans and removed them, her shoes and socks soon followed suit to enable him to inspect her ankle. He let out a low whistle, wow that looked really bad. His respect for the now sleeping woman increased, she must have been in a lot pain for a long while.

He tucked her in first removing her wet jacket and jumper, and then made a hot drink.

"What to do?" he thought. the nearest place to stop was a hundred miles away.

He was looking at the map, when she stirred

He went over to her, taking a steaming cup of tea with him, "Here" he said helping her sit up, "drink this, it always seems to help me."

She took the offered cup and him a smile that seemed to light up the cabin. "Thanks" she said, "sorry to be such a pain." She tried to move and winced as the pain hit her, also wincing at the fact that she had just realized that she had lost some of her clothing.

He smiled, "sorry but you were so wet, I thought it better" he stopped as she grinned at him. "No matter" she said and again that smile played around the edges of her mouth. He made sure she was ok, before making his way back on deck; the smile she had given him seemed to fill his mind as he sorted out the course for the next town. His thoughts were only stopped when a crash came from below, quickly he rushed down. "Sorry" she said, "I was trying to help."

She was out of bed, and attempting to wash the dishes, but standing on one leg in a boat, no matter how gently the rocking was is not easy.

Before he knew it, he swept her into his arms, and dumped her, gently back in the bed.

"Hey Miss Stubborn, get some rest, those things can wait"

She pouted a very charming pout, it's not Miss Stubborn, it's Wendy actually, but you can call me Genie and no I will not tell you why"

She stuck her tongue out at him, and laughing he went back on deck.

When he came down some time later she was fast asleep.

He sat watching her, as she gently snored and realized just how beautiful she really was. Her face was angelic. Her body though half hidden by the blankets was all that a man could dream of. He already he knew of her bravery and humor. He smiled, and thought to himself, she was some girl this Genie was.

The night passed slowly, he tucked himself into the stern of the boat watching the night skies and the stars that all good sailors know to love, he sipped at the flask of strong coffee he had prepared earlier, and started to think of what he should do. He must drop Genie off and have her ankle looked at, but part of him wanted her to be there with him. As dawn started to kiss the sky, his tired salt covered eyes told him it was time to rest.

He set the boat on auto pilot, and went below, falling into the spare bunk his eyes shut before his head ever hit the pillow. He was woken some time later by the smell of bacon being cooked and to find a fresh cup of tea waiting by his side. His sleep fuddled brain took a few minutes to take it all in. He looked up to see the smiling face of Genie. Some how she had managed to get some of his spare clothes on, and was walking about with the aid of a broom, looking like something straight out of Treasure Island.

"Awake at last Skipper" she said with that mischievous smile playing round her lips "we are on course, and I thought you might be hungry"

He gobbled down the offered bacon sandwich and drank the tea.

"Just thought I'd say thank you for saving me" she smiled, and in that moment he decided that he did not want her to leave the boat, he wanted her to stay.

Once finished, he helped her up on deck, and they sat together watching the boat carve through the seas, talking about all and nothing. He found out about her, what she had been doing, where she was going, he told her of his plans, and she seemed to listen and take it all in. Eventually he asked her about staying on after her ankle had been looked at.

She smiled that smile then, which outshone any star from the previous night's visage.

"Of course I'd love to say" she answered, and his heart skipped like a spring lamb.

The rest of the day was spent laughing and learning, come mid afternoon they sailed into the harbor. He helped her to the local hospital, where after much waiting, it was found the ankle was not broken just badly sprained. Strapped up with a fresh supply of painkillers and orders from the doctor to rest, they made their way back to the harbor. They sorted out the berthing of her boat, picked up the extra supplies they needed since there were now two of them, and as the sun set in the western sky, slowly the boat sailed out into the moonlit sea.

They settled into a routine, enjoying each other company, and growing closer each night, until as the stars shone down on them one warm still evening. His arms round her, he leant and kissed her, with a kiss that was answered with such power and longing that his breath was completely taken away. Huskily she said "Now I can really thank you for saving me". Taking his hand, she led him to the cabin, where this time, she undressed for him, then removed his clothes.

The moon shone through the cabin door, as they found each other, with a love and passion that neither of them expected, but both desired. Bodies met and molded, hearts sung together in a duet of love to the sea and the sky. Cries of love and passion were lost on the nights wings, until as the dawn once more broke; they both knew that this was a different voyage. It was a voyage of love, and of life, something that from that day on they would sail together.

SALT WATER LOVE PART 2

The sun beat down on the smooth glass-like ocean, hardly a wave rustled the smoothness, it was hard to tell where the sea ended and the sky began. The morning heat haze was just starting to leave the sea. I did not move want to move, everything was so peaceful and I just did not feel like moving.

My mind was going back many years to one of my earliest sailing days. The day in fact, that I had first met my Wendy. What a time that had been, rescuing my Wendy after her boat had been hit by the wash of a tanker. Leaving her in such pain and yet still she was able to sail the boat until I had found and rescued her.

That had been the start. We had fallen in love and sailed the seas together. First as lovers, then after a beautiful ceremony, on a Jamaican island, as man and wife.

My Wendy had been with me ever since, our lives had been full of happiness. We managed to work and sail splitting the year into equal halves. We both worked so hard, knowing that the money would enable us to sail into the sunset for 6 months of heaven. We had been to most places on the seven seas and had many adventures, some of which my Wendy had written about in a book, which even now, as I lay here under the sun, was being published.

We had, with the money that we hoped the book would bring us, planned our most ambitious trip, selling even our house to furnish the cost of a new boat. As well as everything else that was needed for this adventure from England to Australia.

It was some journey and unlike all the boats that you read about in the famous races, or people tackling the trip `single-handed', we were doing it for fun. We aimed to stop wherever we wanted, whenever we wanted and to enjoy every mile. All the planning was completed and on a windy, dull English day, we set sail on our adventure.

The journey had been fantastic, we were, as on that first journey we made together so in love. We shared the tasks, the chores and the pleasure. Every day had seen something new, something different. Small fishing ports full of friendly fishermen, big bustling cities. But at the end of the day, there was just Wendy and I on our boat, our own island in the huge ocean.

Things went well until we got to the Indian Ocean; here we had been hit by a typhoon that had come at us out off nowhere. Our brave boat battled for days against the pounding seas. My Wendy and I fought the seas day and night, we barley ate or slept. Working as a team, we had seen the sun disappear not to be seen again for several days. Then, just as the worst was over, just as we thought we were finally going to get some rest, at the darkest time of the night, something hit the boat. Whether it was a whale or a container washed over the side of a boat, we never knew. Water flooded in through the hole in the side of the boat and we grabbed what we could and started to prepare to abandon ship. The sea however had one final trick up its sleeve. Just as we were ready to leave the boat a fresh wave must have hit us. One moment we were slowly sinking, the next I was in the water with no sign of the boat or my Wendy.

I do not know how long I swam around that spot; the seas as if satisfied by the sinking of the boat became calm. I called and yelled until my throat became raw with the effort and the salt water. My heart died in that instant and I think I did too. Eventually I swam across a large piece of our boat now all smashed and pulled myself on board.

Stories from the Heart

The sun came out and lit the sea, plenty of flotsam from the wrecked boat floated around me in the now still waters, but there was no sign of my Wendy.

Days came and went, until now here I was laying on my wreckage raft under the hot sun, remembering the woman I loved with all my heart and who had now left me.

As the sun created the haze over the sea, I looked deep into the water and saw the face of my Wendy. She was smiling up at me, reaching her hand out to me. Telling me to come home to her, our home where we had first met, the sea.

Without thinking and not able to stand, I rolled off the raft and with a smile on my face as bright as the sun that beat down on me; I slipped into the arms of my love. As the waves closed over my head, I was once more with my Wendy, this time forever...

Storyheart

THE WINDOW

The last dying rays of the sun caught the tear drops as the slowly ran down the face looking out the window. The threatening rain clouds that had shrouded the sun during the day had gone, and the red tint of the dying sun now lit the evening sky with a pinkish hue.

Though the sky was clear, the face of the woman was covered in clouds, and thunderstorms of tears streamed down her face.

This was the day he would have arrived, the ship was due she told herself, words she had muttered every day the last week, he would be there. She continued to look out the window, there was no sign of the ship, and no news had been heard for some time. She looked and hoped she wished and prayed, and she waited. The house waited, ready to greet its master and her husband on his return. Instead there was a pale tear stained face that looked through the window, and waited, as she had done for the last week, empty, lonely days, waiting him as she would forever.

Her man would return one day, but the window and the woman knew in their hearts that he would not.

~~*~~

A face pressed up against the glass, small hands drawing pictures in the steamed drawing surface of the window. Excitement filled the frame and small hands and eyes tried hard to look for the expected visitor. She had been there for a long while, or so it seemed to her, but still there was no sign.

Stories from the Heart

She once again hurried on the window, and wrote in small childish script "ANNA". She prided herself at the way she could write her name. Once again she turned back to the window, and pressed her small features up against the glass. She had waited so long, but he must be here soon, he must, what would the rest of the day be like if he didn't come, she let out a little sob.

Once again, she looked to through the window pane, was that him?

She brushed her arm across the window, and looked again. Yes, yes he was there coming down the street, heading for her house. He looked up at her face pressed against the glass, and shrugged, starting to walk on. Her heart sank, but he turned and with a huge smile headed for the door.

She rushed to meet him, flinging open the door, and he handed her an armful of cards and gifts. "Happy Birthday Anna" he said. Leaving a smiling 6-year-old, who was enjoying her birthday.

~~*~~

The old lady looked out the window, the glass was dirty and slightly cracked in one corner. The street outside was lit by the gaslight, shadows played along the street, on the passing cabs and cars. A tram rattled down the street, sparks filled the air from the overhead lines. A couple walked by arm in arm, not noticing anything around them, lost in each other, oblivious to the world around them.

The old woman let out a soft sigh. She too had been like that once, she too had loved, had known the feeling of being in love, the wonderful feeling that filled your heart and made every day a new experience. The way just a touch could set your heart racing, the brush of a pair of lips on yours, that made your heart beat that much faster.

She sighed again, where had those days gone? Where was the love that had made her life so special? As she wiped a tear away from her eye, noticing the wrinkled skin on her hands, and sighed again. That was long, long ago,

Storyheart

time will not wait for anybody, and love like a flower can blossom, but also like a flower can grow old, wither and die.

She had lost him a long time ago. He was one of the many that never came back from the Great War. She let out a little laugh, the Great War, so many lost, so many lives changed, and for what.

She once again looked out the window, she felt a pain in her chest, as a glow seemed to fill the sky. She looked up, and the window seemed to disappear before her, and she found herself being drawn towards the light. Suddenly she heard his soft voice.

"I'm here love, I have been waiting so long for you, but now you're here and we will be together for ever."

She reached out, taking his hand, noticing that hers were no longer wrinkled, he was as the day they had gotten married, young, handsome, and oh how she loved him. There would be no more looking out of the window, they were together now and forever.

~~*~~

He looked out the window, the glass painted black, to protect them through the blackout, tape crisscrossed the pains to protect the people in the old house from flying glass in case of bomb explosions. The radio crackled behind him, news of the Dunkirk and the evacuation was the main news, and he half listened as his he looked through the window.

His son was over there, on one of the flotillas of small boats that rushed to answer the call to rescue the army from the beaches of France. He had wanted to go, pleaded to go, but his son had reminded him that with only one leg, it was not really the place for him to be, when so many lives depended on them.

So here he was waiting and hoping. The news told of dive-bombers and many lost boats, of bravery above and beyond anything that could ever be imagined.

He looked once more and his vision blurred, from the darkening skies or from the tears that now filled his eyes.

There was his son, slowly making his way down the road, looking so tired, head bandaged, but he was there. The old man turned and let the tears flow. Before recovering the window with the blackout curtains, and making his way to the door, to welcome his son, home safe and sound.

~~*~~

The last dying rays of the sun caught the tears drops as they slowly ran down the face looking out the window. The threatening rain clouds that had shrouded the sun during the day had gone, and the red tint of the dying sun now lit the evening sky with a pinkish hue. Though the sky was clear, the face of the woman was covered in clouds, and thunderstorms of tears streamed down her face.

She waited, looking through the window, he had been gone so long, the war was over, and there were tales of prisoners being repatriated, every day on the news. She had not heard any news for so long, but she waited and hoped. Then only this morning she had received a letter dated many weeks before. He was coming home, he was actually coming home. She never read any more of the letter then, her eyes would not let her and she could not read because of the curtain of tears that covered her vision.

So now here she was here face pressed against the old glass of the window. How may others have looked out the window she wondered how many others had waited and hoped? Her mind was brought back to reality by a knock on the door.

She looked out the window; a stranger was standing outside the door. But as he turned around, her heart caught in her mouth, not a stranger, it was him. There after all this time. Tears of happiness, filled her eyes and she rushed to the door and into his arms, the wait was finally over.

Storyheart

A ROSE BY ANY OTHER NAME

It was a glorious summer's day, the day she was born. One of those special days you remember all your life and wonder why they do not happen any more, which of course they still do. Her proud parents knew at once what to call their beautiful daughter, for she stood out like a rose in the garden of all the other babies, a beautiful rose. So that is what they called her

She grew up fast a beautiful, loving and caring daughter, until the girl Rose bloomed into the woman who was Rose. She knew love, and she knew pain, she found that not everything in the garden of life was beautiful. Several weeds that tried to suppress her found that this Rose indeed had sharp thorns.

One day, Rose met the man who was meant to be for her, the love of her life, her soul mate. And on a beautiful spring day when the flowers were fresh in the garden, she married her man; rose petals covered the blooming bride and her man.

Rose knew such happiness, such love, and everything in the garden was wonderful. That was until one day in winter, when the frost ended the beauty that was Rose.

Her husband was coming home late one night, when his car hit an icy patch and skidded off the road. The medics were quick on the scene, but not quick enough to save the life of the only man that there would ever be for Rose.

That night the woman that was Rose started to wither and die, as her heart died with the loss of her love. She was often seen at the roadside where her love had died, every week she would lay a fresh bunch of roses at the spot of his death.

Like a flower though Rose faded, withered and eventually died a broken stem of the beauty she once was.

Even after she died, people swore they saw a woman weeping at the spot where her husband had died, and people who drive by the spot found their cars covered in rose petals.

BATTLE SCARS

Bright lights, like angels filled her eyes, flashing in and out of her vision, shapes whirling, twirling, moving, and fading. Then with a sudden sharpness a person dressed in white beckoned her to follow them. She looked up, ahead was a glow, a warm, welcoming glow that looked safe, and homely. Leading up to it was a corridor of brightness.

The person ahead, turned, and she thought for a moment she knew them, there was something familiar about them, and yet she could not quite put her finger on just who it was and how she knew.

Again the figure ahead beckoned her, and she started to put one foot in front of the other, moving up towards the light from the darkness that was below her.

Something in her mind knew she must get there, knew this was where she needed to go. Her head whirled, vision flashed in front of her eyes, but she kept moving up and up, following the smiling figure, until suddenly she burst out as a fresh light filled her eyes.

Slowly she began to focus, and shapes became clearer, a voice, soft, reassuring was saying something to her, and she could feel her hand being held. Yet it was not her hand, something was different.

Slowly things became clear, she was in a room, a very white room, the face of the person cleared, and that of a nurse came into focus. Slowly she understood the words the nurse had been saying to her. It was all right, she was safe, and that for a moment they had almost lost her, but she was back now and safe.

She tried to move her hand, but it was bandaged, and held down, the effort made her flinch. The room started to sway and the face of the nurse started to float before her

Stories from the Heart

eyes, as once more the darkness took her. This time though, it was the restful land of sleep that overcame her.

Where had it started? She tried to think, as she lay in the ward, slowly recovering a few days later. Her mind worked back through the tapestry of the last few days, or was it weeks or months. Like a film on rewind pictures came and went until a day several months before when the moving backwards stopped and the film started to roll forward.

She was there, and so was he. The man she had longed for, the person who was there, filling her life with a joy she had never thought was possible, her life, her soul mate. She was so happy, theirs was a marriage made in heaven, she was so happy, and every day she was so thankful that he was part of her life.

She thought. Had she missed something then? Had she been so blinded, blinded by love to miss the signs of what was to come? She tried to think. There were times that the smile had slipped from his face, there were moments when his thoughts seemed to have been far away. What had he been thinking about? She put it down to pressure of work. Something in her even thought it could be another woman! She had laughed at that.

"As if" she had said to herself.

The truth though, she now knew.

The pictures slowly moved on, days came and went, and now she could see the change that came over him, the look of worry that crossed his face. He had even disappeared for several days without telling her where he was going. Then one night he did not come home, calling her, telling her he had been sent on a business trip, but now she knew otherwise.

The film stopped and the horror of the picture faded away as sleeps wings wrapped round her, numbing her to the last picture that had filled her mind.

She awoke, sweat covered her body, and pain filled her mind. She must go on, she thought, she had to fight to get

Storyheart

through it, to battle through these last pictures that until now her mind seemed unable to cope with.

Slowly, she went back and once again the film began to roll, this time she noticed other things. The look of pain that flicked across his face, the times she caught him looking at her with what she swore was a tear in his eye.

Then, one day she came home, and he was not there, she thought nothing of it to start with but as the hours went by she began to worry. Then that sound, that still sent chills down her spine, and fresh tears to her eyes. The sound of the phone had made her jump; she rushed to it expecting to hear his voice, telling her he was on his way home. Instead however it had been the voice of a woman, a voice and a message that sent her rushing from the house, tears streaming down her face. How she drove she would never know, as the rain on the car windows matched that of the tears that filled her eyes. She parked the car and jumped out rushing towards the entrance, where was he, she had received a call, he was here, where was he?

She was lead into a room, and he was there, she let out a cry as she remembered how he looked.

He tried to smile as he saw her, and reached up to have her grasp his hand, love filled his eyes, and he forced out the words to tell her how much he loved her, each one being an effort. As if now at peace, and still holding her hand his eyes closed, this for the last time. As she held his hand she felt it turn slowly cold in hers, slowly she bent and kissed him.

After the crying had stopped, when his body had been taken from her, when her heart had stopped breaking she had been told by the doctors exactly what had happened. How he had been ill for a long-time, gradually getting worse. How he would not let them tell her, and the effort he had made to keep his illness from her, even to the time he had to stay in hospital for a night. They then gave her a letter he had written.

She went out into the now sunlight, without knowing where she was going, found herself in a park, where they had shared many happy moments together.

She sat on the still damp grass and opened the letter; her eyes read words that she never knew could exist, as he poured his heart out to her. Painting a picture of his love for her, telling her over and over again how much she meant to him. He told her of his plans, for her, how he had taken steps to make sure she would be all right. He begged her to forgive him for leaving her this way. The words seemed to run into each other, as did the days after that. She did not know what or how things took place, but they did. The funeral, the insurance and the house, everything had been taken care off.

From that day onwards she had died, each day was filled with pain, with longing. She was losing the battle.

She just could not live without him, could not face the lonely days and the ever so lonely nights, she could not exist. Then one day she decided that was enough, if she could not be with him here then there was nothing left to keep her on this earth, the battle was lost.

It was all in slow motion; she took pills, and then with tears in her eyes, cut her wrists and sat watching as the life blood seeped from her body. That was the last thing she could remember until waking in the hospital.

She held up bandaged wrists, she now knew the face of the person who had lead her towards the light, it was her man as he looked on the day they had met. She knew what he was trying to tell her. That she must be able to face what life would throw at her, and that he would be there with her always. She would fight she thought, for them both, she would fight for their love.

She looked once more at her bandaged wrists.
She would wear her battle scars with pride!

THE AIRPORT

She sat at the table in the airport lounge, slowly sipping from a cup of now lukewarm coffee. Remnants of an airport sandwich, not digestible at the best of times, lay before her.

She looked out the window and saw nothing but a gray mass of nothing. Everything was grounded by the gray fog that had rolled in several hours ago and looked like it was here to stay.

She looked at the woman who looked back at her from the window. She looked tired, her but her blue eyes twinkled in the reflection. No wonder she looked tired, it had been a long, long day. Here she was not going anywhere, just watching the hands on the clock slowly tick away the seconds.

She looked again at the reflection, and brushed away a straggling strand of blond hair from her face, once again resetting the ponytail that held the rest of her hair in some resemblance of order. Her eyes again gave that slight twinkle and a faint smile spread across her lips. He had said her eyes were the first things that had attracted him to her. She laughed at that and the reflection laughed with her. Was it all those months ago they had met? She looked out the window again, her mind drifting back to their first meeting.

It had been a glorious sunny day on the West Indian Island, she had been resting beside the pool, soaking up the rays. She had not noticed him that was, until he fell over her, spilling his ice cold drink on her in the process. She had jumped up forgetting the undone top part of her bikini, which did not jump up with her. Her eyes! She laughed; his had nearly popped out of his head when she had sat up like that.

They had started talking then, once she had sorted her attire out, a talk that went on for the rest of the day. That night they had gone out together, they had danced talked and kissed until the sun started to rise in the early morning sky. They had walked along the beach, two sets of foot prints in the pink tinged dawn light. Then a final kiss, and the knowledge that this was something special.

The rest of the holiday went by in a dream of happiness, days and later nights in each others arms as indeed they were filling each others hearts. Learning about each other as only lovers can do.

All too soon it was time for her to leave. Her eyes had taken days to recover from the tear drops that were shed that day and her heart even longer.

Now, here she was in a fog bound airport.

She finished her last dregs of coffee. "Oh well" she said to herself, no more trips for her for now; it was time to get back to work.

And after work, she smiled, he would be there waiting for her as he always was at the end of her shift, to take her back to their new home.

Both of them had found the love that was meant to be for them on that holiday.

And now they were together forever.

THE KNIGHT AND HIS LADY

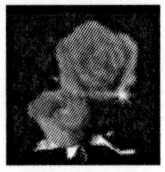

Part I

She did not know what made her decide to go for a ride that morning, but suddenly a thought, a flash, something came to her and she decided to go for a ride. Calling for the stables to saddle the horse, and asking her maid to hurry and change as they were going for a ride. Before long the two women were galloping across the green country side.

The lady felt wonderful, the wind played with her hair like a lost lover, the horse moved effortlessly beneath her, and she laughed with the happiness of the ride, the sun, the country, the sheer thrill of it all.

After some time, the maid called, asking if they could please stop, as her mount could not keep up with her Lady's fine white mare. Reluctantly the Lady reined in her horse until the mare stood panting, ready to answer her mistresses' slightest touch to once more leap into motion again.

The Lady looked around, this part of the woods were not familiar to her, but they knew the direction of the castle that was the Lady's home, and slowly set off in the general direction. Letting the horses make their own speed, allowing them to stop and eat when ever they wanted along the way, the Lady and her maid, chatting as though they were best friends rather than a Lady and her maid, which in truth they were. The woods soon rang to the tinkling laughter of the two young women, but suddenly came to a stop as the two entered a sunlit glade.

There before them, were several bodies of what looked like robbers and in the middle an armored figure lay, like a tumbled heap of scrap iron. With one glance the Lady knew what had happened, the robbers had set upon the knight. She looked around counting the number of bodies on the ground. He had put up a very good fight against many adversaries; quickly she drove the thought from her mind and moved to inspect the knight.

This was nothing new for the Lady as she had for some time, much to the amazement of her family been studying the art of medicine. She wanted all to be able to bring relief and nursing to all people not just the rich, as was the current state. She had seen so many charlatans and false doctors in her 19 years, so she had decided many years before what she wanted to do with her life.

Bending over, she lifted the helmet from the knight, and gasped at the blood soaked face that lay before her. The maid swooned, but the Lady with a sharp command ordered her to fetch water from their travel packs, and stop being such a milksop.

Gently she bathed the face of the knight, revealing his young and handsome face, marked by lines that spoke of laughter rather than frowns. The eyes gently fluttered and opened, revealing a pair of blue eyes, which seemed to focus on her own before once more closing. She inspected the knight for injuries, he had suffered many cuts and bruises from cudgel and sword thrust, but she could find nothing life threatening.

She must take him back to the castle, where he could be tended to until he was well, she smiled to herself that could be interesting, and let out a little giggle. Recovering she looked around for the knights sword, which she found broken on the ground. Her respect grew with the knowledge that he had fought on, even with a broken sword. Taking the blade, she bid her maid help to her while she cut two stout branches, which with the aid of some rope found on one of the robbers, they bound the branches together with some smaller limbs until a form of sledge was made. This they then harnessed to the Lady's own horse.

Then with both of them being as gentle as they could they half-lifted half dragged the knight onto the sledge, he moaned but did not wake.

Then slowly, trying to avoid any bump that she could the Lady led her horse slowly home, sending the maid on ahead to prepare the castle to receive her charge.

~~*~~

Part II

Upon reaching the castle, the Lady ordered the knight to be gently taken to her own chambers, where without any waiting she set to work removing the knight's armor, revealing a fine young body covered by many bruises and several old deep scars. Eventually after bathing and wrapping the knight in fresh sheets, she forced a juice of fresh herbs into the knight's mouth, She settled down to watch over the knight as his breathing turned to gentle sounds of sleep.

Every so often she leaned over and bathed the knight's head, holding his hand as he thrashed about moaning as the fever in him reached its height

Days passed with the Lady hardly stirring from the bed of the knight and then one morning a weak voice woke her from her dosing.

"Where am I?" mumbled the knight each, word taking a supreme effort.

"Hush" replied the Lady, soothing his brow with a damp cloth.

"You are safe, and amongst friends"

The knight seemed to relax

"Am I dead? Are you an angel?"

She giggled, "No Sir Knight, you are not dead, though for some time there it was touch and go, now rest. The worst is past and you must regain your strength".

Stories from the Heart

Suddenly the knight realized he was naked underneath the covers. He tried to sit up, but at once fell back gasping. "Did you?" he began to gasp, but the words were lost as once more Morvias closed his eyes.

Days passed and the knight grew stronger, the Lady came every day to visit. Each time telling him stories about her day and what had happened.

How the cook had broken the best pot. How the stable boy had fallen in the horse dung. How the flowers were blooming in the palace garden. Gradually, the knights' spirit began to return, his laughter joining hers at her latest tales of palace life, and day by day she began to find out more and more about him.

They learned more about each other in those few weeks, than most people do in a life time. They told each other their deepest secrets, their plans, their wishes and their dreams.

As the knight grew stronger, she walked with him around the palace, the gardens, showing him her world, enjoying their time together. At last the knight was well enough to leave her, and though she never said anything, she knew that her heart would break, when he did.

No word of love had passed either of their lips, nothing more than the holding of a hand to aid the other as they walked or rode through the green countryside.

At last, the time came. The knight put on his armor, now fresh and cleaned, and prepared to say his good-byes.

The Lady stood, at the castle gate, trying so hard to be brave, as the knight took her hand and gently raised it to his lips.

"Sweet Lady, I owe you my life, and will always be in debt to you. But there is something I must do before I leave you, something I must say"

She stood there watching as he hurried off into the distance, her lip started to tremble. Suddenly thinking what was happening, suddenly realizing just how much the knight had begun to mean to her.

Storyheart

She turned wiping a tear from her eye, letting out a sob that can only come from a broken heart. Not seeing any person as she rushed to the castle, not caring who she ran into, who she knocked into, just wanting to be alone, to go back to her room, and forget the world in a sea of tears.

She stayed in her room for two days, and refused all attempts to bring her from her room of sadness.

~~*~~

PART III

It was on the third day that she saw a man striding across the courtyard, heading towards her room. It was only as he came near that she realized it was her knight, no longer clothed in armor, just in plain doublet and hose. Moments later a knock came on her door.

"Go away" she said with a timid voice, "Please, Sir Knight, go away" The knocking came louder.

"Lady let me in, I have to see you" came the voice she had last heard saying those words of goodbye.

Slowly she walked across the room to open the door, but at the last moment something stopped her, and in a quiet voice she said "Please, Sir Knight, go away I beg you"

The knocking stopped and she heard a sigh followed by footsteps moving away from her door.

A week later the Lady ventured once more into the world, though her face showed no sign, her heart was aching fit to burst With her maid she wandered around the market, picking up items without really seeing what they were and not intending to buy anything. Her mind was numb, as was her heart, and it was only when she suddenly felt an urgent tugging on her sleeve from her maid that she realized they had stopped in the middle of the town square. There before them was a small ring in which two men were fighting toe to toe, one man was a huge giant of a creature, whose fists the size of mallets was reigning blows upon a smaller man. Who's only defense seemed to be his quickness, for he was managing to avoid most of the blows. Blood covered the smaller man from many cuts, and she

Stories from the Heart

turned away at the sight of even more blood, a sharp pain piercing her heart at the remembrance of what had gone on before. She was just about to go, when a gasp from her maid, made her turn.

She looked again, even now the smaller man was fighting back, but wait, her heart flipped, her mouth dropped, that face under the blood, she knew the eyes, the smile, it was her knight.

~~*~~

PART IV

The world seemed to spin before her as the roar of the crowd echoed in her ears, and suddenly she was falling into a black pit of darkness.

She felt herself struggling, climbing, then the hazy forms appeared before her eyes, and as they cleared, the worried, blood smeared face of her knight slowly focused. She went to move but the knight hushed her. "My Lady, please don't trouble your self, it is me, and I am fine" The knight gave her a smile that rocked her heart until she thought it would break once again.

Slowly she sat up with the help of her knight.

"Please my Knight, take me from here" she whispered clinging to the fact that this was all a dream.

He swept her up in his arms and with a glance to her maid, to let her know all was well, strode away to a special place they both knew of. He settled her down on a mossy bank, under the spread of a willow tree.

"You left" she began "Why are you here? Where is your armor?"

He quieted her with a kiss, and she thought her heart would fill her chest to over flowing.

"My Lady, when I left, I told you I had something to do, and so I had. I decided that all I ever wanted in this world was her, the love of the most beautiful, kind, wonderful person in the world, you my Lady"

His face split into a grin

"I had nothing to give you except for myself, so I went and sold my armor and my sword, and purchased this ring."

He slowly pulled a cord from beneath his shirt "With which to ask you to make me the happiest man in the world" he put the ring back. Sighing he continued "When I came to ask you my Lady, you refused to see me, what was I to do, I had nothing, so I helped round the village, and made some money at the boxing booth in the fair. Oh! I won by the way" he said with a grin, and clinked some coins in his pocket.

Suddenly all became clear to the Lady, what had she done, nearly lost everything, through one misunderstanding. Her head felt light, and her heart pounded in her chest.

"Oh my knight I am so sorry" she started to utter, but this was quickly quieted by a kiss that she had longed to feel again for these past few days. The kiss went on and on, until time itself seemed to stand still.

At last they parted and she rested her head in the arms of the man she loved.

"What was the question you wanted to ask me that day you came to my room, and I did not answer you" she asked with a grin.

The knight moved until he was kneeling before her.

"Lady, I am but a poor knight who has nothing to give you but my love, my life, my soul and my whole being"

She smiled at his discomfort "I am nothing without you my Lady, so please my love, will you" He stuttered, then once again started in a firmer voice, sure that this time all would be right.

"Would you my Lady, do me the honor of becoming my bride", at which he pulled the ring from cord around his neck and offered it to the Lady.

Smiling with blue gray eyes lit like fireflies the Lady took the ring, and placed it on her finger.

"My knight, with all my heart I say, YES, YES, YES, but first please just call me Jade, for that is my name"

"My Lady Jade" the knight replied.

The rest of the words being lost in a kiss that lasted through the happiness of the rest of their lives together

Storyheart

LONESOME DOVE

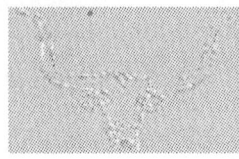

For the umpteenth time that day the wagon got stuck in the gripping mud and for the umpteenth time that day she wondered what she was doing here alone in a wagon. With a mixed up, ragtag bunch of pioneers, following some long ago lost trial, in the wind and rain. The dripping of the rain from the wagon canvas seemed to know exactly where the gap in her slicker was. Each drop finding its way down her back.

It had of course not started out like this. She remembered with a lump in her throat how she and her parents had set off to discover the Promised Land, "Go west" the signs had said, and that's where they had headed. Sadly it was just a few weeks into their journey that a freak flash flood in a box canyon had taken several wagons and their owners to a Promised Land far beyond the American shores. Her parents had been two of the people lost that night.

Of course the rest of the wagon train had offered every kind of help they could, expecting her to turn around and head back east at any moment. She was made of more steel than they thought, and carried on, single handed across the miles heading for whom knows what or where.

Though her parents had always called her their "little bird", she had soon become known to the rest of the wagon train as Golden Dove.

Because of her long golden hair, which in those early days could be seen flowing behind her, as she kept pace with the wagon train on her horse.

Stories from the Heart

After the death of her parents, she cropped her curls, and the people soon started to call her Lonesome Dove instead.

At last the wagons slowed down, forming into a muddy circle to rest for the night. Lonesome Dove, slowly climbed down from the wagon, and wearily started to sort out the supplies, that they might need. Shifting through the soaking packages trying to find something that may help with tonight's meal.

The other folks were all very quiet, with the not only the weather dampening their spirits but the fact that none of them were exactly sure where they were. The wagon master who had started with them on their trek had been having been another poor soul that they had lost in the flash flood.

The cooking was done centrally. Each wagon helping boast contents of the meal, and taking it in turn with the cooking and the other chores. Tonight Lonesome Dove was taking her turn in finding wood for the fire, this in the pouring rain was no easy matter, she moved further and further away in her quest for dry wood. All of a sudden a movement caught the corner of her eye, her heart jumped to her throat, before she could scream a warning, a deep voice disturbed the sound of the rain.

"Evening, Ma'am"

Her scream stopped jammed in her throat.

A tall horseman slowly moved his horse from under a nearby tree to stand in front of her.

"Not a nice evening to be out looking for wood"

She looked up into his face that was suddenly lit by a brilliant smile, and her heart stopped trying to get into her mouth and did a little flip.

Some minutes later, Lonesome Dove entered the wagon circle, with some dripping pieces of wood, followed but a tall dark stranger. The other members of the wagon train gathered around the stranger, who was soon joining their evening meal and hearing about the problems that had hit the pioneers so far. He waited until they had finished, then slowly got to his feet.

"Seems like you folks have had a real bad time, and the fact that you are here miles from the trail proves that you need my help. My name is Todd, Todd Bennett, I'm a Ranger, helping out where I can. If you will let me, I'll gladly lead you to the nearest town, where you can hire a scout to take you the rest of the way."

Todd said no more, and as it became clear from the rest of their journey to the nearest town, many days drive away, was some speech from the quiet Ranger. Each day as they traveled, it seemed to Lonesome Dove that Todd seemed to spend extra time riding beside her wagon, giving her that flashing smile, and gradually making her forget her troubled months, even the weather seemed to brighten up.

Every evening it was with Lonesome Dove that Todd drank his coffee, listening to her stories about the east coast, her home, her family and her dreams.

After many adventures, trials and troubles, the wagon train eventually wound it's way into the town of New Grove, where the families set about sorting their life's out, each very grateful to Todd and knowing that without his help and guidance none of them would have survived the journey.

The months passed and when the spring came, the wagon train complete with a new guide and wagon master set out West once more. Except for Lonesome Dove, she stayed where her heart was, safe in the arms of Todd.

The west was tough, and untamed, life for Todd and Lonesome Dove was not easy but together they took all that was sent to test them in their stride, and soon the two became three when their son was born. Todd built them a cabin near a gentle stream, where they made their life together. But the wildness was never far away, and as the town grew, Todd the ranger, became Todd the lawman.

One fateful day, what were three became two. Todd was shot in the back while patrolling the town streets, many fingers were pointed at the killer. But no proof was

Stories from the Heart

ever brought forward. So Lonesome Dove was once more, on her own, this time though with a young son to support.

Winters, storms, floods and droughts, all came and went, Lonesome Dove worked day and night to provide for her and her son. She was known and respected by all and every one, and though she seemed to have got over the loss of her man. In only a few years her once golden hair had turned gray, and though she smiled in the daily work, the pleasure she had watching her son grow, her heart was still crying from the loss of her Todd.

The years went by and her young son grew into a man. It was part pride and part horror that she had experienced when her son arrived home one day wearing the self same sheriffs badge that Todd had once worn.

A year later a message arrived at the town, the man that had shot Todd had robbed a bank up north, and was now heading towards the border. The only law that could stop him was the son of Lonesome Dove.

A showdown happened that very day, and many stories were told about how the young sheriff, was taken by surprise, and would have been shot in the back like his father, except a shot rang out from a near-by alley-way, and the murdering bushwhacker, lay dead in the dust.

Nobody knew where the shot had come from, or who had pulled the trigger.

Nobody knew that is exccpt Lonesome Dove, the woman who would not lose her son, as she had lost her husband.

Storyheart

THE CHAMPION

The hot sun beat down on the field, crowds moved around mingling with the noise of the music and the sights and sounds of the fair. Children ran among the throng, trailing balloons, and heading for who knows where or just wanting to run. Above the noise came the sounds of horses, cows, and sheep all mingling with the general hubbub that was the county fair.

He was swept along with the crowd. The sights and sounds were all strange to him, for this was not his country, and the local fairs in England were nothing like this one. Still it was what he was meant to be doing during his year off from college. This was meant to be a period of discovery, learning about the rest of the world, and enjoying life.

He had been travelling around America for some months working here and there having many interesting encounters, and making many friends.

Now here he was one of the large crowds in a small town in Ohio. It was not like a fair, back home in England, more like a cross between a farm show and a rodeo.

He sat in an empty seat, ready to watch the entertainment, his eyes taking in the color and excitement of the spectacle. His gaze was drawn to the people getting ready for some sort of horseback race. And a flash of a smile caught his eye and an arrow shot straight though his heart. It only seemed to last a moment though his heart seemed to try and tell him something that he couldn't quite make out.

He had seen rodeo events on the television back home, but nothing could compare to being there as he was now, with all of the excitement and the colors. The steer and bronco riding, the calf roping, each was one mass of color and excitement. Then the races started. First the wagon races, which he thought was like stock car races with legs. Then, came the horse rider events, they were like the pony club races back home, but twice the speed and excitement. The riders had to ride fast around a course, sharply turning around barrels at certain points. He suddenly looked up, there in the next race, was the girl he has seen before. Again, he caught the flash of her smile, and his heart tried to tell him something once again.

He pushed down to the edge of the ring. As the race started, his mouth gaped, she was wonderful, seemingly as one with the horse, riding hard then turning so sharply around the barrel. He found himself cheering for her, and when she crossed the finish line let out such a yell that she turned around in her saddle and gave him such a smile that his heart nearly exploded.

After watching the presentation, he made his way to where the riders were cleaning and feeding their mounts. He spotted her at the end of the line, trophy in hand, chatting to several people; he waited until she had finished talking before he moved across to her.

"You were fantastic," he said, not sure what else to say.

She turned and flashed him that smile again, this time his heart just exploded.

"Thank you" she said, "I heard you cheering for me out there"

He blushed and she giggled, "No problem, your accent isn't exactly like the rest of the folk around here"

They chatted for a while, but all he could see were her eyes and her smile.

Suddenly she stopped and looked at her watch, "I have to go, but there is a BBQ tonight. Are you going?"

He did not know what to say, he attempted to start several times, before stumbling out "Yes. Will you be there?"

"Of course" she replied "I'll even save you a dance."

She leaned forward and gave him a kiss, and then with a laugh, she turned and led her horse back to the stables.

He watched her leave, unable to move, not wanting to move, his fingers slowly came to his lips where the softness of her kiss still tingled.

He suddenly came to, a BBQ! This evening!

And she would be there!

He dashed back to his room at the small hotel he was staying at, and tried to find something to wear. Traveling around made keeping clothes fit to wear almost impossible. Still come that evening he looked in the mirror and saw a tanned, well-muscled body, with his fair hair showing off his blue eyes. The reflection smiled back at him, yes he would do.

After asking a few people for directions, he found his way to the BBQ. It was crowded, music of all sorts filled the air, and people of all ages were dancing to all the various beats. He wandered around, was she going to be here? Would he find her in this crowd? He didn't even know her name, after all.

Suddenly there she was before him, smiling that smile that drove laser like arrows through his heart.

She grabbed his hand and dragged him off to a small table on which sat giant punchbowl.

"Here" she giggled "you look like you need one of these." Taking the glass from her and realized that she still had hold of his hand or did he have a hold of hers.

They wandered around the BBQ, listening, talking, dancing, and just learning about each other.

Her name was Jean, he liked the sound that. They sat listening to the music late into the evening, watching the dancers moving in the moons silver sheen.

Their arms went around each other and he tasted the lips that made his whole world turn upside down. The night sky was filled with fireworks, but the kiss left him gasping at the power of the emotions that over took him.

They sat for the rest of the night until the first hint of a pink tint appeared in the sky. They talked, they kissed they just sat and held each other. By the time the first rays of the sun lit the east, they knew all about each other, their hearts had become entwined, as had their lives.

He walked her home, and kissed her gently goodnight, before reluctantly leaving to go back to his room and grab what sleep he could. He would see her that evening, it was the semi-finals, and she was riding.

He woke, not sure if last night was a dream or not, but the tingle on his lips, and the feeling in his heart told him it had all been true. Dipping into his depleting money reserve, he went down to the stores, he had an idea. Knights of old used to carry their lady's favors into battle. Perhaps he thought she could do that for him. So he found a moonlight blue bandanna, which he tucked into his pocket and headed back to the fair.

She was there waiting for him and rushed to meet him as soon as she saw him approaching She kissed him with a conviction that took his breath away and showed him that last night had been sweet reality and she felt the same way he did. He gave Jean the bandanna, and explained about knights and lady's favors. She laughed and immediately placed the scarf round her neck.

"There you go," she said, "I am now your champion, and will be riding just for you." She said the last part quietly as if trying to tell him something, or so he thought.

Kissing him once again, she ran off to get ready for the race. He pushed his way through the crowds to get a place right next to the finish line and waited for the race to start. This time, the excitement of the rodeo and the wagon races did not affect him. His mind was churning, as he started to realize what was happening to him. He was meant to be moving on in a few days. He already had plans for the next part of his journey, and had booked his Greyhound bus to take him to his next destination. Now after only twenty four hours he wanted to stay here, wanted to stay with Jean, wanted to enjoy those tender kisses for the rest of his life.

At last the horse races started, again he marveled at the sheer grace and speed of the riders, Jean seemed to move as one with her horse, and the excitement filled him again as she easily won her heats and was heading into the final. He was still standing there watching the other riders, and thinking over the way his life was going, when a pair of hands covered his eyes. To be shortly followed by a kiss from a pair of lips that made all thoughts of moving on disappear.

"Well did your champion do you proud?" Came a soft voice that sent shivers up his spine.

He turned and hugged her to him "You were wonderful" he said hugging her again, and realizing that he wanted her very badly, "Do you have to race any more?"

She smiled "No." She said "That's it, I'm in tomorrow's finals" she giggled," but I have other plans for the rest of the day."

She took him down the road towards her farm and then along a winding path that led them deep into the woods. Sunlight dappled through the branches above them and bird and insect noises gently filled the air. Hands held tight, he found her leading him into a small glade deep in the woods.

She looked into his eyes, a shy smile lighting up her angelic face.

"This is my own special place" she said "nobody else knows about it, but I wanted to share it with you" she bit her lip, then slowly continued "I want it to be our place, and I want this place to share what we are about to do"

He gasped, what was she saying? Could it be? Was it his dream coming true?

He took her hand and led her over to a small bank, she seemed a bit unsure, as was he, but she suddenly seemed to make a decision. She flung her arms around him, and kissed him until he gasped for breath.

Stories from the Heart

Slowly, he lowered her to the ground, for the rest only the trees and the animals of the forest were witness to. They went into the woods as people new to love, and came out as lovers.

The rest of the day went by all too fast, they were now together, and all of his plans had now changed, he never wanted to leave her. Later that night as he kissed her goodnight at her house, he told her that he loved her, and with a kiss and a flash of that smile that lit his life, she told him she loved him too.

The finals were the next day. He kissed her good luck, noticing she had his bandanna on just to show she was his. The races went by until it was her final. He was as nervous as she was, and watched as the race started, she went off fast as she had done before, this time though the others went with her, at each barrel turn she seemed to gain slightly as once again Jean and her horse seemed to move as one.

With a final turn she set off for the finishing line, she was leading by about a length when there was an audible snap, and her saddle started to slip from her horse.

He gasped, as she tried to stay on the horse, just crossing the finishing line before plunging to the ground.

His heart stopped and before he knew it he was over the boundary. He didn't care about the other horses or riders and rushed to where Jean now lay still, unmoving. He knelt by her side, and gently held her, as others rushed to help, her eyes fluttered and opened and she tried to smile, her hand weakly moving to her bandanna. "See," she muttered "I am still your champion."

Her eyes closed, and he was ushered out of the way by the first aid team.

He went with her in the ambulance, sitting with her and holding her hand, telling her it would be all right, hoping she could hear him, though she was unconscious all the while.

He sat and waited while the doctors took care of her, meeting her family as they rushed in to see what had happened. He sat beside her bed. And although she was still unconscious, he talked to her, he told her how much he loved her, he told her about the way he never wanted to leave her, he told her about his past, he told her the plans for their future.

Her family came and went, they had known about him from things she had told them. Soon they realized what they had become to each other and welcomed him into their family.

In the end, they forced the red eyed Englishman to come back with them to their home in order to get some sleep.

Hours turned into days, each day he was there, he never stopped talking to her, holding her hand, and just being there for her. Then one morning as he lifted her hand and once more, as he had done so many times before he kissed it. Her eyes slowly fluttered and opened.

He was just about to call out for the nurse when something made him stop. She was trying to say something to him. He leant forward and gently kissed her. She softly said.... I LOVE YOU, before once more closing her eyes, this time though into a gentle sleep.

He stumbled to the door to call the medical staff, and then to let her family know that she was conscious, and would be all right. And more than that, she loved him, and their future together was already starting.

Taking a greyhound ticket from his pocket, he slowly tore it up; he would not need it anymore. He had a very special reason to stay, after all he was in love with a champion and she was in love with him.

Stories from the Heart

THE OFFICE

It was another day at the office. He sat at his desk wading through the reams of computer printouts, his fingers every now and then making a tip tap sound across the computer keyboard. His work was not exciting but it was a job. He earned enough to enjoy life; he had his own flat and was able to live his life as he wanted to. Yes, it was a job, but it was dull, dull, dull.

He completed yet another bug fix, and once again ran the program he had been working on. If it worked this time he thought he'd take a break. Perhaps go and treat himself to a cup of tea or even nip out to the sandwich bar down the street and get one of those huge cream cakes. He hit the run button and watched the program go through the various steps, there were a few warnings, but these could be cleared later. It went through and with a final "Completed Successful" message at the end, it finished

Right he thought, a cup of tea it is, closing the folder of printout, he locked his screen and headed towards the floor below, where the new coffee machine had just been installed. It was further away than the one on his floor, but the tea out of it was at least drinkable.

He was fishing in his pocket for some change not noticing where he was going when he bumped into a form bending down to retrieve a cup of some liquid from the machine. He gasped an apology as the face of the startled woman bending over the machine gave him a look of pure anger. Her drink had splashed all over her. Again he mumbled an apology, noticing though that she was new a person one he had not seen before. He thought he knew the entire list of good looking woman in the company, after all he was single and the Christmas parties at the office were famous for relationships, or so he had been told. However the parties he had attended were pretty tame.

He picked up his tea, and made his way back to his desk noticing as he did so that it was time for lunch. He got back into the office and by the emptiness of the department realized that most of the others had gone to the pub for a liquid lunch. He sipped his tea and seated himself at the computer, still he thought it would give him some time to go and chat, as chatting on the internet was something he liked to do at lunchtime rather than go down to the pub.

He logged on, and entered his normal chat room, signing on as "Britblue" the handle he used when chatting. Several of the regulars were there, both male and female, and he spent some time having merry banter with them all. A new name appeared, Lost Angel, it was her first time in the chat room, and he like the others made her feel welcome. While he chatted to her, something made the hairs at the back of his neck stand on end, he shivered, must be a draft. He went through the normal business when meeting a new person, finding out her "stats" as it was called.

She was around his age and sounded pretty good. He enjoyed her humor, and typed away merrily until the noise coming from the lift told him the others were coming back from the pub.

The next few days he seemed to spend more and more time chatting to Lost Angel, and found his chat changing from hugs to kisses. To his joy he found that unlike many of the others she was actually in England, though he did not know where, and she seemed reluctant to tell him.

The weeks turned into months, and Christmas loomed on the horizon and the company Christmas party. He should go to the party he told Lost Angel, one lunchtime. Just to show his face, but he was not sure how long he would stay. Lost Angel agreed, her own work's do was the same night, and she thought the same.

Stories from the Heart

He had been trying to make arrangements to meet his Angel for some time, but she seemed unsure about meeting a person in real life that she had met chatting on the net. Their times together had become physical, all be it in a cyber way, both knowing what pleased the other.

The night of the party, he made a presence; there was plenty of laughter and jokes, even to somebody actually providing some music, which as the evening went on people, actually began to dance to. He had intended to leave mid-evening, but as the drink went down and the music got louder, he actually found himself enjoying the evening.

His evening seemed to get even better we he spotted the girl he had bumped into those months ago at the tea machine, and noticed for the first time, how good she looked. Charged with liquid courage and the spirit of Christmas, he made his way over to her and started talking to her. He found her utterly charming, and soon they were getting along as if they had known each other for a long time. Her name was Michelle and she worked in the account office on the floor below. She made him laugh, and laughed with him, and as the evening went on they danced, held each other, and as the last record faded into the night he kissed her, and found his heart suddenly beating like a sledge hammer.

He took her home, kissing her once more as he said goodnight, hands did not want to part, but she told him no when he asked about a coffee, she laughed.

"Last time we had coffee, you made me spill mine" laughing she kissed him one last time and before he could answer she had skipped away, and with a final "see you," disappeared into the doorway.

He made his way home, not sure of his emotions, he was feeling something he had never felt before, and did not know what to do. He needed to talk to somebody, he needed to speak to Lost Angel.

The next morning being a Saturday he was up and checking his email hoping to see his Angel in the chartroom. He was pleased to see the light flashing on his PC telling him there was fresh mail, and when he checked found it to be from Lost Angel.

She was full of herself, bubbling over with excitement, like him she had met a person at her works party, she spent paragraphs going on about how tender and kind he was, how he had made her laugh and the feeling she got when he had kissed her.

He was a little jealous, but understood after all he had met somebody to. She had asked him to meet her in the chat room, that evening, he replied to her telling her his own story about the person he had met and how his heart had not stopped since he had met her, arranged to meet her that night.

Throughout the day his mind wandered to Michelle, she seemed like he had known her forever, they had seemed so natural together.

Come the evening Lost Angel was already in the chat room, and before he could start telling her his news, she was telling him all about the wonderful person she too had met.

As the evening went on, something seemed to be sounding bells in the back of his brain, and she suddenly stopped typing and left him wondering where she had gone.

Suddenly it hit him, the description of the party, the things they had told each other about the person they had found, why they hadn't spotted it before.

She sent him a private mail message, "Is it, are you?, was it?" she didn't know what to say, neither did he.

Again the message came to his screen, call me please and a phone number followed this, something Lost Angel had never given him before.

He disconnected from the net, and dialed the number, a quiet trembling voice answered the phone.

"Hello" said the soft voice and his heart flipped in his chest

"Michelle?" he asked

"You" she said, "it really was you!"

He did not know if she was happy, sad or what, the voice went quiet and he thought he heard a faint sob.

"Michelle, you're Lost Angel, aren't you?"

" A faint laugh came from the phone "None other"

They both laughed and started to talk at the same time, the telephone call lasted four hours, and neither could remember what was said.

They agreed to meet the next evening at a local pub, they laughed and joked about the Christmas party and how they had been telling each other about the person they had met, without knowing they had been talking about each other. The evening went and the conversation-quietened, gaps of silence appeared in their conversation.

Suddenly Michelle stood up, "this is ridiculous," she said and grabbing him by the hand dragged him, uncomplaining out the door. They moved along the road, not saying a word, and this time she did not stop outside her flat but opened the door and pushed him in.

"Look" she said when they had entered her small home "We know each other better than this, we have loved each other many times, we know how things are, we know what each other likes, and we know how we feel about each other"

He did not say a word, just nodded his head in agreement.

"Now" she said "Come here and kiss me"

He went to kiss her and suddenly had an idea, they had always typed things to each other before, and that apart from the Christmas party, that is how they knew each other best.

As he went to kiss her he started talking as if he was typing.

"Moving forward I kiss your soft and tender lips" he said, moving until he kissed Michelle's lips.

She understood at once and joined in.

Storyheart

"Feeling your lips on mine, remembering the touch of them, and the love you show me" she said, kissing him back.

"Tenderly kissing you" he continued

"Feeling you in my arms and wanting you" she replied

"Wanting, and needing you" he slowly said, looking at her.

She kissed him, and looked into his eyes, "Then take me darling, take me as you have done so often on the net, love me as you know I need to be loved"

They started that night to do with each other as they had talked about so often. The loved, they gave each other what they had dreamed of for so long, adding to it with every movement of their bodies and every beat of their hearts.

After that, their love never stopped growing; people at the office did not know why they both had huge grins on their faces.

Their love knew no bounds, they sat next to each other at her home, and their PC's just touching, as were they.

Themselves, the kissing the touching, the feeling enacted the words that they had typed. The typing stopped as their loving started as they reached highs they never knew had existed.

Nobody knew until yet another collection made its way around the office, when people checked as to who this one was for, the names of the two people who were getting married were Britblue and Lost Angel.

Stories from the Heart

BAR ROOM HEARTACHE

He sat on the bar stool, sipping the last dregs from the glass in front of him. He was trying to make it last, trying not to have to dig into his pocket and buy another drink. It was a case of time against beer. He looked at the clock ten minutes until closing time, then back at his almost empty glass. "Sod It" he said, and swallowed the last dregs, catching the barmaids eye he ordered another beer. Surely he thought there must be something more than this, he sighed, well there used to be. Once, there had been laughter and love.

His fresh drink arrived, and as he sipped it, his mind flowed back to what had happened not too long ago.

Was it only a month, he sighed, his life had been so happy, she was there and everything was wonderful. Sure they had their ups and downs, but then who didn't. He did not see the signs, did not notice the hurt looks, the sadness in her eyes, or the looks that flashed across her face. Others did and tried to tell him, but he just wanted to be one of the boys, and took her far, far too much for granted.

Then, one day she wasn't there, he did not think much of it, but then she was not there the next night either. So he called her, and she did not return his call. Folks in the bar, whose comments he had not listened to, told him what a fool he had been. He called the next night, and the next, but she still did not answer, or return his calls.

Storyheart

Finally he realized what he had done, and that it was over. The bottom had fallen out of his world.

He lost it that day, lost his will, his heart, his soul, he also lost several days, and nobody would ever tell him afterwards just what he had done during those dark days of despair.

He heard later, that she had found another, and that she was happy. This made him smile, if she was happy, then that was ok. After all, he had his seat at the bar, and his friends, and of course everyone thought all was ok, as he laughed and joined in with the banter. But some knew he also had loneliness and a heart and a heart that would take a long time to mend.

Sighing once more he finished his drink, said his goodbyes to the folks in the bar, and set off to his lonely empty house once more, where his broken heart would cry about what head done. In taking her for granted.

INJURED LOVE

The tear slowly slipped down her face, leaving a dirty trail across her cheek. Today was the day; he would finally be coming home.

It had seemed a lifetime that he had been away. Her heart skipped as she remembered the day she had first taken him to hospital. She remembered the look in his eyes that day, so helpless, so alone; he had been in so much pain.

She had visited him as often as she could after that, each time leaving him had torn her heart, until it was in shreds.

That was several weeks ago, now here she was, and after all the pain and suffering he would soon be there with her once more. Soon, so very soon, she would hold him in her arms, and gaze into his deep brown eyes, and see the love there.

The doorbell rang and there he was, with that same old look on his face and the same eyes lighting up at the sight of her. She took him carefully in her arms, not wanting to hurt the freshly scarred body. He kissed her face, and a wet tongue let her know he was home.

She took him into the house, and placed him tenderly on the rug, she loved her dog, he was everything to her, and now he was finally home again.

ANGEL CAKE

Raindrops splashed against the window, the rhythmic sweep, sweeping of the wiper blades attempting to
Keep the window in front of him clean. Music from some unknown radio station seemed to mix with the blade beat and the steady purr of the engine.

Again, he strained to look ahead, where the hell was he?

He had lost his route almost an hour ago, he was sure he should have found the town he was meant to be staying in by now.

A light ahead caught his attention; he slowed and found himself outside a small and welcoming diner. He suddenly felt tired and hungry.

He got out of the car and made a rush for the diner's door, entering with a squall of rain. He shook himself off and looked around, it was small but welcoming place, and he once he felt better. He felt warm and welcomed, there weren't any flashing lights or neon signs here. A jukebox in the corner was playing old songs from his youth. Without thinking, the words formed in his mind and his hand tapped the beat on the counter.

"Ok, ok" came a soft voice from the back of the kitchen from which a wonderful smell now filled his senses. "I'm coming, no need to bang on the counter so"

He looked up as a figure appeared as if by magic, and a smile seemed to fill the room.

Stories from the Heart

"Now" said the voice that sent ripples down his spine, "what can I get you?"

He could not answer her for he was lost in a pair of brilliant blue, blue eyes that sparkled a thousand words, without saying a single thing.

"Oh" said the voice of the vision "coffee is it?"

Without thinking he sipped the freshly poured steaming cup that she had placed before him. It tasted so good. Shaking himself, he stammered out a "thank you".

"You're welcome" she said, "we don't get many folk stopping here, so any conversation is better than none at all"

She swayed to the music "I love this song" she said "would you like to dance?"

He did not remember her coming from behind the counter, or even standing up himself, but the next moment she was in his arms and the music filled his veins. The record seemed to last forever, or so he wished. She filled his arms and his senses, her body molded to his like they were two pieces of a jigsaw puzzle. Time seemed to stand still with her in his arms.

She pulled away as the record ended, not without first leaving a kiss on his lips that sent his heart leaping around his chest.

"You must be hungry" she said appearing behind the counter again and pouring him a fresh cup of coffee. "I can understand, traveling on a night like this must be no fun at all"

She disappeared back into the kitchen, returning with a wonderful looking piece of cake.

"Here" she said, "I've just made some Angel Cake. Would you like to try some?"

He tasted the cake, it was as light as a feather and wonderfully sweet, and it made him feel warm and revived, ready in fact, to restart his journey.

He went to offer her payment before he left. She smiled that smile again. "One more dance and we'll call it even" she said.

Storyheart

As they danced he held her as close as he could, each part of her touching him, and making him feel more alive than he had ever felt before. They moved as one with the music, and he knew as the record stopped and they kissed, that he would return.

As he moved to the door, he looked back "I'll be back in the morning" he said with a smile, "for another dance, and some more cake."

The look she gave him brought sunshine to his heart and removed any thoughts of the rain he was just about to return to.

He started the car his mind in a whirl, his taste buds still full of the sweetness of her Angel Cake, and his lips with the softness of her kiss.

As he drove around the next bend in the road a police car blocked his path. An officer rain streaming from his face came over to his window.

"You can't go down this way Sir" he said "the rain has washed half the mountain onto the roadway, and any poor soul traveling along this road tonight wouldn't stand a chance.

"That was a close thing then" he replied "If I had not stopped at the diner round the corner; I would have been on that same stretch of road"

The officer gave him a quizzical look "What diner?" he asked

"The one back there" he replied, "just back down the road, with this road blocked I'm going back there now for some more Angel Cake from an Angel."

The officer sniffed "Have you been drinking sir? There is not a diner for over forty miles that way"

He turned the car around trying to understand what the policeman had said. But there was nothing where the diner had been, he drove up and down the road but still there had been nothing.

Had something happened to him that night? If he had not have stopped, he'd have been on the road when it had been hit by the mountain slide.

He would never know, though the thought and the evening filled his mind for the rest of his life.

No matter how hard he tried, all he could remember was the taste of Angel Cake, and a pair of brilliant blue eyes.

THE 14th MAN

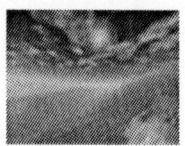

It was one of those wonderful days that only occur in between summer and autumn. The soft sun of the summer, mixed with the gentle chill that heralded the coming of winter through the ever-changing shades of autumn. Even the hard sidewalks of the big city that she knew so well, did not feel so cold. Life was not so scary, and there was hope in her step as she enterred the cyber cafe for her normal chat with friends, and some much needed warmth.

She had passed "hello's" to the normal crowd whom spend time on the worlds internet highway and was herself settling in for conversation with her friends from all over the world, let alone the country. "Friends with no faces" she called them.

Her thoughts were interrupted by the arrival of her best friend, and at once she knew something was wrong.

Mikie was her friend, but more than that, he was her mentor And had it not been for the fact that they were both interested in the same sex, things would have been something far, far more. He had been the reason she had managed to get her life back in order after the death of her other dearest friend. He was the one who had taught her to look up, to aim for the stars and together they had planned to get their lives back in order. He was the reason she lived each day to see the sun, and the person who lit her darkest hours... Yes, he was much, much more than a friend.

But, this day she knew something was wrong, she had not seen him for several days, and had worried about him. Mikie's face was even more gray than he normally was, his eyes, normal sparkling with life, were dull and red rimmed.

Stories from the Heart

"I need to talk with you" he had said.

But gave no reason and she knew it was something she needed to hear, almost as much as she was scared to hear it.

They walked to the park, and sat on a bench the sun light dappling through the spiraling leaves as they fell from the trees. He turned to her and tried to force a smile, and then as the ground seemed to open up beneath her, he told her of his illness.

He told her of this disease that would soon be ending his life, and with that her mind shrieked with fear, not again, not again it kept saying to her. She could not deal with the thought of yet another friend leaving her.

They sat in the park until the first silver beams of the moon replaced the pale sunlight. They talked, they hugged and they cried. He told her that no matter what she would be ok and that he would always be there with her. He made her promise that she would keep reaching for the stars, looking up, climbing up, no matter how many times she slipped. He promised that he would be there supporting her, but she must live for the both of them. She must reach those stars.

As they walked back arm in arm, a strange peace filled her, knowing he had told her, and only guessing how much of an effort that had took. Her resolve to keep her promise to him became stronger than ever. And as she kissed him good night, she knew that her life would go on, and that he would always be there with her.

That had been several weeks ago, several weeks in which they had crammed all that they could of being together and filling their lives with each other. Then this morning, she had been told what she knew, what they both knew would happen. This morning, he had not woken from his drugged induced sleep. This morning he had left all the pain that had wracked his body these past few weeks.

She shed tears, her heart ached, but her resolve was there, and his words keep her strength through a very hard day.

Storyheart

They had planned to go out that evening. She had two tickets to go and see David Copperfield, the magician. He had been so excited at the thought, and they had talked about it for many hours. She knew she had to go, she had to fulfill what she knew was his wish, she had to keep climbing and keep reaching for those stars.

But she also knew, that if she sat there with an empty seat next to her, she would break down, every time she looked at it. Knowing it was Mikie's and remembering that he was gone

She spoke to a friend of theirs, and explained the situation. Andy understood and said that he would go with her, hold her hand, try and be there as Mikie had always been there for her.

The show went by and she managed to bite her lip every time a tear started to fill her eyes at the thought of the man, she had just lost.

Then for the final trick, the magician asked for thirteen men to come up on the stage, and with a final flourish he made them all disappear.

The applause died down, and the lights came up. She had sat there a smile on her lips. Andy turned and looked at her, a puzzled look came across his face. "Did you not see?" she said "Did you not see?" He gave her another puzzled look.

She took his hand in hers. "Andy did you not see?, There were not thirteen men on that stage, there were fourteen.

Andy, I saw Mikie there. He was there and smiling at me, straight at me" Her voice choked and she gripped Andy's hand tighter. "Andy, Mikie was there, he was the fourteenth man, and as he vanished with the others, he looked straight at me, and told me the pain was gone, and that he was going to a far better place. He made me promise once more, and then he was gone"

Andy had looked at her once more, he took her hand and lead her, smiling from the theater

She knew she would never forget Mikie, he would always be there for her, helping her. She would climb that hill and reach for those stars, and keep the promise she had made to the fourteenth man.

~~*~~

Unlike most of my stories, this one is basically true, based on one of friends, and her life.

One of our "Friends with no faces"

THE DREAM

He stirred and half-waking felt without touching, the body there beside him. For a moment, panic set in, where was he? His mind tumbled and with his waking, the knowledge flooded back to him.

He felt the softness and the warmth of the velvet skin touching his, sending little electric shocks through his wakening nerves and smiled to himself at the sweet aching he felt in his body. His thoughts breaking through night's fog, about what had happened the night before.

It had all been like a dream, a play being acted out in slow motion. Was it only yesterday after all this time that he had landed in the place he had only dreamed about? He had looked into those eyes, now covered by sleeps shutters, but bright sparkling orbs of sunshine when she had looked at him; he had been lost in the sunshine he had only dreamed about. Then down to her soft velvet lips that tasted like the honey of the gods, which up until now had been just wishes in his well of dreams.

Sheets, crumpled like white clouds tossed in the ocean of a summer's sky, only half covered the body next to him, flung in the wild abandonment of their lovemaking. The evening had been one of discovery, each wanting to take the other higher and higher. He had given all he could and then found more, she had roused him, driven him, giving him in return for each act the love and caring that only she could give.

At last they had laid there, gently kissing each other, whispering words that meant nothing but said everything until they were lost into each others mouths as again they kissed. Until, at last, still wrapped in each other arms, night's cobwebs had claimed them.

He had woken several times at her stirring, each time feeling the world was his, as the feel of her softness in his arms, and the gentle breathing of her contentment. She snuggled up against him, his arm curled around her, wanting to never let her go, holding her where she belonged. She stirred and gently called his name, her eyes opened, those amber eyes, like twin suns shining with the love and care that had been just in his dreams until now.

He moved to kiss her once more, and his fingers started to trace down her body, as she reached for him and...something hit his head!..bursting the images of his dream

He opened his eyes, angry at being woken from his day dream, wanting to know what happened next. Squinting against the summer sun, it took him a few seconds to realize where he was. The beach, the sea, his holiday, it all came back to him... just as he wished his dream would.

He was startled and looked around to see what had woken him, when his vision was filled with a pair of shapely female legs. His eyes moved slowly up across a body better than any dream, passed a beach ball, which obviously had been the cause of his waking, and into a pair of eyes that smiled down at him.

The vision smiled, with a smile that out shone the summer sun, "Sorry about the ball hitting you, I hope it did not wake you from anything interesting?" She laughed and his heart did a gentle leap in his chest.

He smiled, as did she, and he lost himself in those eyes, bright amber eyes, like twin suns.

Perhaps it was not a dream after all, he thought, but a vision, a snap shot of the future, only time would tell, but this was a good start.

Storyheart

HAND IN HAND

I woke with a start, my body was shaking and covered in sweat. For a moment I did not know or remember where I was. The room, the bed, everything was strange. A hand gently touched mine, and I knew everything.

I had been out running one day, something that seemed to happen every so often. Perhaps it was guilt at those numerous working lunches, or the worry of growing old. Whatever! The shorts were on and I was huffing and puffing along the country lanes. The day was fair, and the thought of the shower followed by a cold beer upon my return kept me plodding along.

A car overtook me, and I had a brief glimpse of a mop of golden hair and a pair of blue eyes as it disappeared around the corner.

Suddenly the quiet of the morning was pierced by the screeching of brakes, followed by an almighty crash

As if it were a starting gun, the sound of the crash sent me racing round the corner, to be confronted by a tangled mass of metal.

It would seem from the first glance, a farmer was coming out of one of the fields on his tractor, when the car came around the corner, hitting it fair and square.

I rushed to the wrecked vehicles. The farmer had been thrown from the tractor and was now slowly getting to his feet, blood streaming from a deep gash in his head. He mumbled something about a farm and the ambulance, and started off unsteadily across the fields to a distant house.

I went to the car, the smell of petrol filled, my senses. I reached inside the car, trying not to move the man who sat behind the wheel turned off the engine

Stories from the Heart

I did not think about what might happen if another car happened to come along.

I needed to try and free the man, his eyes flicked open. He tried to speak, but blood spilled from his mouth.

"Do not bother with me" he gasped "I've had it. Save her, save my Diane"

I looked into the back of the car, the blond mass of curls was very still.

"Diane, it's ok, I'm here, its ok"

A hand grasped mine, and in that brief moment, I lost my heart.

That hand never left mine, all the way through the ambulance journey, and into the hospital.

The days that followed as I sat at her bedside, that hand was often in mine. The driver was dead when the ambulance arrived, and though everybody tried, nobody could be found who was related in anyway to my Diane, as that is how I now looked at her.

So here I was sitting by her bed, and that hand was once more in mine. This time though I felt a gentle squeeze. And my eyes filled with tears

Oh well I thought, perhaps I was not too old.

I settled back in the chair, a hand small and soft in mine.

Tomorrow I thought, tomorrow, I would see what had to be done to take care of the small angel that lay there in the bed. After all, she would need a father now and I knew that no matter what, I had just found a daughter.

FOREVER

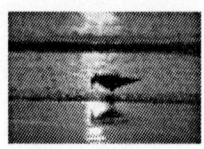

She turned and walked away, her footsteps making an eerie sound on the cold airport floor. She must not look back, she could not look back. She knew that if she did she would lose it, she would let the ache, the pain, and the shear terror, overcome her. Her heart was torn into a million tattered pieces, yet just a few hours ago it had been singing, flying amongst the clouds of love, entwined with that of the man she loved. She knew that if she turned around now, he would be standing there, that if she turned he would never leave, and yet they both knew he had to go. So she continued to will one foot in front of the over and walked away.

She got into the car and went to turn on the engine, the sound of a jet engine starting up made her hand stop just before the ignition key, and she lost it. All the pain all the tears came flooding out, her vision distorted by all her tears, she was numb, aching and heart broken.

How long she sat there she did not know, her face was blotched, and tears had been streaming from her now reddened eyes. She could not drive, she was shaking, and she was so, so lonely. She took out from her pocket the last gift he had pressed into her hand just before she turned away she opened the small box and found a delicate heart-shaped locket. She took it out and opened it, revealing the engraving inside "Forever" it said, and once more the sheet of tears covered her vision.

A long while later she finally started off home, driving automatically, her thoughts with a man flying ever further away from her, and a heart ache that almost stopped the breath filling her chest.

She got home, entering the door almost expecting him to be there, welcoming her as he done the couple of days that she had gone to work while he was their. She sat down fingering the locket, thinking of the time they had spent together.

Remembering the touch of his lips still on hers, the warmth of his body as they lay side by side, the tenderness of their loving, and the heat of their passion. But now he was gone.

The days went by, they talked and they talked, but it was not the same, he was not there with her. Often at night or working through the day she held the heart locked and pictured his eyes smiling at her, and knew that they would be together one day. And each time she realized it would not be for some time and the heart ache and loneliness started once more. She lived for their phone calls, scanned the net for his emails, and ached with every fiber of her body to hold him again.

Christmas, the New year, went by and if anything the missing and the ache got even worse, some nights she swore in her half asleep moments he was there holding her. She could feel his warmth beside her, smell that masculine smell that aroused her body, then she turned and realized he was not there.

As the days went by February came and one day a beautiful bouquet of flowers was delivered to her door, with it was a note with words that only he could have written. Words that brought back the tears that had covered her face that night when he had left her. That night she wept, hugging her locket to her heart, wishing with all and everything he was there to take this loneliness away from her.

The next morning she woke her eyes were still red, she stumbled down the stairs, it was Valentines Day. She expected a card from him, and that would have to do until later that day when she would hear his voice on the phone. She fished in the mailbox, and sure enough there was a card with the writing she knew so well on it. Slowly she

Storyheart

made her way back to the house, not wanting to open the card until she was inside, knowing that there would be tears once again. She sat down and looked at the letter, her sleep starved brain slowly realizing there was something wrong with the address.

It came to her in a flash, yet puzzled her, there was no stamp on the letter! Slowly she turned the envelope over, written on the back were the letters DBH, what the heck did that mean?, DBH? All at once she was awake, throwing the letter down she rushed to the door. Her heart pounding DBH, Delivered by Hand, Delivered by Hand! She threw open the door and there he was, arms open, and a smile as big as the distance that had previously separated them. Again the tears came this time from happiness, she sobbed into his shoulder, and he kept telling her, that he was home, he was home.

This was her valentine's gift, a gift she would never forget. He like her had found he could not live without her, and now he was there. This time there would be no tears, no goodbyes, this time he was home, and it would be forever.

PURRRRFECT LOVE

I first met her when I started college, right from the start she stood out from the rest of the crowd, her black hair that almost used to shine. Her green eyes that could flash a smile, and then like the weather of her Scottish homeland, change in an instant to be full of storms and lightning. But mostly it was her pure presence, her grace, the almost feline way she used to walk around. Though her name was Kirsty, she soon got the name of Cleo from her beauty and cat like presence.

We spent a lot of time together, but I was just one of the people who tried to share there life with Cleo, men were like bee's round a honey pot with her, she always had them queuing to be with her. Some ended with smiles like a cat who has had some cream, others found that the cat had claws and came away with a different point of view.

But all the time she was there, her green eyes flashing, and her beauty out shining the stars in the sky. I spent some time with her, but knew I could never be one of the chosen ones. Perhaps because of that we became friends, and spent more time, just talking about things, and being there for each other when milk got spilt and hearts got broken. One thing about Cleo, was her appetite for adventure. Each year she came back from her travels with some new adventure, some new happening, and normally a new scar to add to the few that already marked her from her travels during her year off from college.

She had been bitten by a snake in Africa, and had only just made it to the missionary's medical center to get some antidote. She had been surfing off the coast of Australia, when a shark had attacked the person surfing next to her.

The first summer at college she came back telling tales of her travels across America during the summer and how she got caught up in a robbery at a bank in some small town. Gunfire had filled the air, a bullet snatched her earring, from her ear and left a scar across her lobe. She talked to me about the trip and I spent many an hour listening to her paint the pictures with her soft Scottish burr.

And so it went on, each year something different each summer brought another adventure for her.

I remember our graduation, and the way she looked at the ball afterwards, wearing, well almost wearing a dress as black as her shining hair, she was a queen that night, and men came to pay homage to her. I will never forget though she made sure that I had at least one dance with her.

After college we went our separate ways, Cleo and I. We passed the odd letter, and I found that her life had not changed. Several times in her adventures had me thinking how lucky she had been, and how close she had been to death. A ship sank under her in the Greek Islands and she gotten caught up in a terrorist attack in the Far East.

Then one day we met quite by chance, I knew as soon as I saw a dark haired beauty glide into the room, that it was Cleo. Her hair was still black and shining, her face now tanned, and her eyes lit the room. The grace, the poise, oh yes it was her. She caught me looking at her and a smile lit her face when she recognized me. We sat there for hours, telling each other of our lives, feeling at home with each other like we were still at college. I loved hearing her talk of her adventures. There had been several more brushes with death, but she just smiled. "After all" she said "she was a cat and had nine lives". We arranged to meet again, the following day.

That night the comment about the nine lives kept going around in my head. I counted the stories, the near misses

Stories from the Heart

so to speak, and realized that she had used eight of her nine lives. The rest of the night I could not sleep.

The next day I had met her, and being a non-workday had been with her all day.

That was the start, when we finally became a couple, soon lovers, and then she moved in with me, and we became "us".

Now though, the ninth life was there, the last life, but this time, that life would be wrapped in my protecting arms. I knew like a cat, she would need her time alone, and need her space. But I would be there waiting for her, knowing she was mine at the end of the day, and loving her.

The knot that was tied on that day of our wedding would keep her safe, this may be her final life, but it was also a new beginning for the both of us.

Storyheart

THE PRECIOUS GIFT

Like a drowning man, reaching out towards the sunlight above him, he dragged himself from the nights clinging mire. Slowly surfacing into reality from the land of dreams, his senses gradually coming back to him.

Where was he? It started to come back to him as he broke through the Sandman's cobwebs of sleep.

Sometimes it was hard to know what country he was in, let alone, the location.

His sleep befuddled mind, like a film just starting gradually slipped into focus. Thoughts rushing through his mind of the last year

He had left his home, his county that he loved, left his family and his friends. Left everything he had ever known. Heading West as the people had done hundreds of years before. To start a new life in The Promised Land.

As with the early settlers, he had taken very little with him, leaving so many memories and dreams behind.

There had been times in those first few months, and in fact there still were, when he wanted to give it all up, and just crawl into a corner. There were times his head would say "Enough is enough, I can't take any more". The last few years of his life had been such a roller coaster ride of emotions. Days and weeks filled with dark despair or heights of happiness. Helped by faceless friends, whom had been there through his very darkest hours.

He always said a silent prayer to those people

With their help he had gotten through it, each day another step along the road to happiness, to the star that was his future. Always there were pitfalls and moments of despair.

He remembered some nights he had spent shrouded by curtains of tears, not sure how or if he could go on, but he had gotten through them.

He glanced at the clock; it was 3:26 in the morning. The quiet of the night almost ready to welcome the first sounds of the day, the first fingers of dawns golden glow just starting to show in the East.

Sighing again, he thought what had gone before. Was he right to do all he had?

He had made many mistakes on his life's journey, was this another one?

A small sound brought him back to reality, reminding him of why he was awake at this hour.

Leaving his warm bed, his dreams like ships scattered by a storm, left strewn upon nights wings. He moved towards the sound, and a pair of deep blue eyes reflected the soft silver glow of the moon, looked up at him. As he bent down a very small hand grasped his finger and passed on a message to him, food was required.

Yes! It had all been worth it, the despair, then pain, the hardship and the worry. Looking down, he looked into the eyes of his reward, his so very special gift.

Tears filled his eyes, this time of happiness. And a warm hand reached to hold his, as he felt the warmth of her standing next to him. The reason he was here, the reason had got through everything. Her scent filled his senses, and his heart skipped a beat as it always did when she was near.

Yes it had been worth everything.

He held her hand, and knew it was just so, so right.

He was with the woman he loved, and together they had produced the most special gift of all, their daughter who now started to let her parents know that she was hungry.

This was the future, this was happiness, and this was love.

Storyheart

THE GOODBYE

I remember the day as we walked to the station, there like a brother trying to be strong for you. Holding your suitcase, with you walking there beside me, not wanting to look at the tears, that I knew were there lying just under the surface of your emotions.

Seeing the redness of your lip as you bit it trying not to let the dam give way and the world to see how you felt. You in your best dress, and me in my work clothes, words could not be said, you were going away. Like a big brother I was there with you, nobody else to say their good byes, I should have put in for a half day, but the thought of you leaving had swept that away from my thoughts.

As we walked, like the fog dissolving under the first rays of the morning sunshine, slowly my cloudy thoughts began to crystallize. You were going away, the person who had been my friend, and my confidant, the girl whom I had seen change into a woman, you were leaving.

The thought of losing your friendship, suddenly disappeared and I knew that what we had was more, so much more than friendship. I looked at your face, pale beneath your summer hat, and knew that I had been blind for so long. My heart jumped realizing that I loved you, and that you had told me in so many ways over the past years just how much you cared for me.

All too soon, we were at the station, on the cold platform, all the words have gone, along with all the plans, the hands of the clock, slowly erasing the moments we still have together. Your hand shaking slowly slips into mine and I know this small instant, I should tell you to stay, tell you not to go, but the words will not come

I hold you in my arms, my heart crying out don't go, don't go, and I see in your eyes the heartache, and then

Stories from the Heart

the discovery as you see my own feelings have finally realized what has been there for so long. That we love each other

You slowly slip away from me climbing onto the train, our finger tips just touching and our lips for the first time, meeting and the huge explosion of feelings that are released with that one tender kiss

In still photographs the train begins its run, and suddenly all the words I should have said fill my mind. The ever smaller dot blurred, and I wipe my eyes feeling the droplets of tears that have suddenly sprung from there.

Leaving the station, numb I had walked back through the park to the bar. I was sitting there some time later, lost in my own deep thoughts only shared with the rim of my beer glass. When the voice on the bar radio announced the fatal train crash.

Like coming out of a dream my tired eyes read the black headlines on the now faded newspaper, held by two old wrinkled hands.

Headlines, that had shouted out the end of my world.

"TRAGIC TRAIN CRASH, MANY KILLED"

So many years ago, and yet that moment of realization was even now so clear in my mind, the discovery, the loss, the heartache. My hands shook, and my breath came in gasps.

"Now, now" said a soft voice, "Put that paper down, you know how much it upsets you"

I looked up into a wrinkled and smiling face, and once more could see that girl in her best dress, as we kissed our last good-byes.

She had gotten off the train at the next station, not able to leave knowing that the love that we had been blind to all this time. She had found me covered by disappear amongst the crowds round the railway station trying to find out news of the train disaster. She had found me and grabbed my hand, as she had done my heart. With no further word being said we had left the noise and the bustle, me unable to fathom that she was actually here.

She held my hand all the way back home that day, as we traced the steps made that morning. Held my hand as the stars lit up the night sky and my dream became reality.

I looked down as her fingers wrapped once again round mine. Held my hand then and forever more.

RIPPLES IN THE POND

He sat there tossing stones at the smooth surface of the pool, and then watched the ever-increasing ripples make gentle waves and patterns. Until at last they reached the place where he sat. It was rather like his life he thought. Everything went smoothly and then from one little disturbance, his whole world was turned upside down.

He reached into his pocket, fishing out the very dirty and much read letter. Opening it he once more read the lines that he knew by heart.

"Dear Love

This is so hard for me to write, but I have to. We have become so deep into each other, and each moment we are apart is such a struggle for the both of us. Our love we have always said is a love that will last forever.
But love, we both know that is just not possible. We live in different worlds, so many miles apart, and our lives will never be able to join as we have talked about so many times. So I must end it now."
He looked at the spot on the letter he swore was a tear stained at this point. Was it hers or his he thought? And then read on.
"We must part before our love breaks us, before the pain of distance tears us asunder, before what we have becomes soiled and dirty. I know this will hurt you as much as it

> ***hurts me to write it. But my love, we need to have lives we are able to live.***
> ***Please forgive me, my love, but it is best for both of us."***

He crumbled the letter once more in his hand when he read the last lines, "best for both of us" How could she have said that? That letter had broken his heart, been the stone that had sent the ripples across the smooth surface of his life.

The first ripple was that he could no longer function after receiving the letter. He tried day and night to speak to her, he tried to write, emailed her, even tried to phone her, but could get no reply.

His work had become second place, and soon he was in trouble there, long nights without sleep, long days without a reason to live, left unable to do anything.

It was not long before he lost his job, and with that the second ripple appeared.

He had no reason to stay where he was, and created a mad plan to go and see her, confront her and ask her to tell him to his face that she no longer cared.

He had packed, and drew out all the money he had left in the bank. After all without her what else was there in his life. He had left all he had and boarded a plane. Ripple on ripple spread as his friends were left wondering, his family just could not understand.

He had traveled for many hours until he had found himself in a strange country, at a strange location, and not knowing what he should do next. In all the rush, and with his mind not being able to function correctly he had not even checked on how he would ever find her.

The plane ticket fell out of the envelope as he tried to put the letter away, and along with it a bus ticket.

His heart had been very heavy, but he knew what he had to do. After he had checked all the possible connections he had found himself on a bus heading deep into the center of the country. He remembered how his heart had seemed to sing to the sound of the wheels, "I'm coming, I'm coming". He had tried once again to call her from the bus station, but again there was no reply.

He held the bus ticket in his hand remembering the pain of each mile, the wanting, and the needing. His heart and gone on a roller coaster of emotions, the fear of rejection, the expectation of finally meeting her, the worry of what she would say, the hope that they would be together. The journey had been lost in time, he had no idea how long it lasted or where they had gone, he just wanted to be where she was.

It had been a hot hazy day when he had finally arrived at the small town, where she lived. Sweat had been running down his face, perhaps from the heat, perhaps with the nerves, and the sudden realization of what he had done.

What would she say. What would he say? He could not just turn up on her doorstep, but then that is just what he had done.

He found a cheap place to stay and washed the trip out of his body, and then slept the first sleep he had managed in many days.

Unable to put things off any longer, as the first tips of the sun sunk into the western sky he found himself outside the door of her house. Twice he had gone to knock on the door; twice he had turned and walked away. Finally he had gone, and walked those last few heart-wrenching steps to her door. Slowly he had knocked on the door, almost in slow motion his hand rising and falling, the sound echoing to the beat of his heart.

He skipped another stone over the water, and watched as more ripples appeared, just like his she had spread so many ripples through his heart.

He had waited there, the whole world seeming to have stood still, waited, and waited, but nobody answered, once more he knocked, louder, in desperation, again and again. Nobody answered the door, nobody came the cry from the heart.

Storyheart

He gazed over the rippling water, remembering his sheer feeling of despair at that moment, his whole body seemed to turn to water, and he had felt himself falling to the floor.

He woke in a hospital, or a bed of what he thought to be a hospital, crisp white sheets, and a smell that only hospitals seem to have. He had slowly looked round the room, his eyes clearing, until they rested on a face looking deep into his eyes.

He had gasped, almost fainting once more, as she was there, her hand holding his, and a look of such love in her eyes, he knew that all had been worthwhile. He had at that time, not notice how pail and drawn, she had been, or the fact she was in a wheelchair.

He had tried to talk, tried to tell her he loved her, tried until the room began to whirl with the effort, but no words had come. His heart had been beating so fast the monitor alarm had started to sound. She had just sat there, tears in her eyes, and a look of such love on her face, sat there, holding his hand, until sleeps wings once more engulfed him.

In the days after that he had found out just why she had written the letter.

She was dieing, it was all to do with some illness with a name he never had managed to pronounce. She had not wanted him to know, to worry, to do anything silly like travel to see her. So that is why she had written to him.

He had spent the next days with her, and all that he had ever wanted to tell her he had, and she had told him, the same. Theirs had been two hearts finally joined as one. But with every passing day she had gotten worse. Until, what must have only been a few days ago, she had finally lost the battle and left him.

He knew it was only for a matter of time, and that soon they would be together again, some day very soon.

The sunlight glittered on the water, and reflected on a single gold band that was on his finger. She had left him,

Stories from the Heart

but not before the hospital Chaplin had pronounced them man and wife.

He looked once more at the widening ripples, which for a moment seemed to increase in size before settling once more to the mirror smooth surface of the lake.

Everything was quiet, and he was with her once more.

Storyheart

THAT FATEFUL DAY

As the first kiss of dawn, touched night's black sky, and caused the world to start wake for another day. In a small room, a lone figure tossed in his bed. Sheets scattered, tossed, like the wave caps of an autumn storm at sea. One arm flung wide across the pillows, his body seemingly unable to keep still, tossed around in the sheets, a film of sweat coating his naked torso. As the first suns rays lit the window, with a cry he woke, dragging his mind from the deep mire of nights dreams.

It had happened again, that same dream, that same feeling of helplessness that had filled his life so many times over the last nights. It seemed like forever, but had only been a short while, since in fact that fateful day.

He rose from the bed shaking and went to the bathroom. The reflection that gazed back from the mirror, shook him. His face was gaunt, haggard, dark circle smudged his eyes, which were red with lack of sleep. A film of sweat covered his forehead. He leant on the sink, as wave after wave of nausea ran through his body, sending his head spinning so he had to hold on for fear of falling.

He gripped the side of the sink until his head cleared, and splashed water over his face to try to stop himself from shaking. He remembered the day, the day he had uttered those words that now had come to haunt him and from today, his life would change.

A knock on the bathroom door made him jerk up, sending his head spinning again. "Hurry up" said a voice "You going to be in there all day?" He stumbled to the door, and opened it to see the smiling face of his best friend, Mike.

"God" Mike said "You look really rough!"

He mumbled some vague obscenity, and stumbled back to his bedroom.

Looking out the window, his eyes half closed against the mornings suns glare, he took some deep breaths and the room finally stopped spinning.

Today was the day, when his would change, though it had really changed since that fateful day he had first asked his love to marry him. Now today was the day, his stag night had been one hell of a night, and he was suffering. But today and he smiled as he pictured his soon to be bride walking down the aisle towards him. But today, it would be all worth while.

Storyheart

THE POOL

We sat at the side of the pool, sunlight reflecting in soft ripples that had appeared there from the last dipping of your toes. Soft sunlight filtered through the tree tops, touching your face, and covering your tanned body with a myriad of different patterns.

Our fingers touched, and memories came back to each of us, when bodies loved, and learned. Reflected in the mirror-like waters, was a couple who had found love in this very special place. The day when we first met. The stumbled opening of what was now a fully developed love. The moment we first discovered this spot, hidden from prying eyes, lost among the trees.

We had fallen in love to the tinkling sound of the waterfall. Shared our love in the silence of the pool. Whispered words under the moons silver beams, which shone like the love in our hearts.

The silence was broken by the cry of a bird, seemingly joining in the shouts of pain that echoed round our hearts

Once more we both looked away as if drawn to the pale shimmering waters, hidden in our own special place. Where lovers had held hands and kissed, as we had ourselves done. Without saying a word, we lent towards each other, knowing what was needed without a word or a signal. Our lips touched in soft sweet kisses, tainted with salt from the tears which shone on your cheeks.

We both knew that today was our last day, the end of a romance, no matter what we might say or promise. Like the waters that ran tumbling down the waterfall into the silent pool beneath, in time, would wash away the rocks. Soon days and distances would wash away our love.

Leaving just the memory of this moment, reflected in the pool of our lives

Storyheart

THE GREEN MIST

I can't remember when the green mist first came into my life. Thinking back, I guess that it had always been there, for as long as I can remember. Always at important times in my life it had appeared and my life had changed in one way or another.

I remember one of my first days at school, playing in the classroom with my best friend Ray. There was one new toy that had arrived in the classroom that week. It was no different to many of the other toys in the classroom, but it was new, so of course we both wanted it. Like all children of 5 or 6 we started to argue over it, and tears came to our eyes. Then, just as the teacher started towards us to sort out the squabble, the green mist came down.

Next thing I can remember is my parent's arriving at school, to take me home. Once there I was sent to my room, and a while later they came to talk to me, to try and explain, and find out what had gone wrong with their normally placid son. They told me, that it had taken three teachers to get me out of the classroom. But like every other time the green mist came down, I could not remember a thing about what had happened.

As I grew up so the mist came and went. The football game where I took on the whole of the opposing team, after being hit by one of them after the whistle had blown. The trip to the coast when I had ended up being left behind after not doing what I was told, the green mist made me deaf as well as blind.

Time passed, and I grew up, and learned to control the green mist. As with every teenager, it was a time of discovery and learning of life and love. I knew happiness and heartache, until at college I finally met the person that I was sure was meant for me. She came into my life, like a breath of fresh air, her smile lit my days and her lips sent me to sleep smiling each night. The mist I thought had disappeared, and everything in my life was wonderful. We were a couple, an item, a pair. We grew into love, as we grew into each other, learning the ways of the body and the heart together.

Plans were made as we graduated and began working, both knowing that our love was all that mattered. Our love was all that we knew. That was until the green mist struck once more, and I lost all I had ever dreamed about.

I met my Bekki after work one day, she had been invited to a friend's leaving party, I did not really want to go, wanting my Bekki all to myself. But she wanted to go so we went. The party was actually quite good and everybody was enjoying themselves. The drink flowed and with each passing hour, the music went up a notch or two. I came back from the bathroom, and was looking for my love, as the slow records had started to play. Suddenly I saw her on the floor, her arms draped around a person she had introduced me to earlier as her boss. His arms and hands were all over her, and then the green mist came. The next thing I knew, I was being pulled away from a now prone, bleeding and unconscious man. The look Bekki gave me was one so full of pain and anger, I could not look her in the eyes.

I turned away and left, left the party, and left the town, left the state. The green mist had cost me all the mattered in my life.

I found a job working as a Forest Ranger, away from all who knew me, and all who could be affected by the green mist. I found peace in the woods, amongst nature, peace and understanding, and gradually I was able to control my feelings, and the green mist. The summer season brought many visitors to the park, and I made many new friends. No more green mist, no more worry, and almost no more heartache.

Some years later, a flash flood warning was broadcast for our forest area, a huge lightening storm was heading straight for us. The park was full of people enjoying their summer, all of which we had to evacuate because of the fast approaching storm. I drove through the forest to one of the more remote picnic areas, when the storm broke. In my time as a Forest Ranger I had seen many storms, but this one was the worst. Suddenly visibility was almost down to zero, huge sheets of lightning flashed across the sky, mixing with the crash of thunder that rolled around the hills. Ahead I could just make out the reflection of a car's taillight, and a fresh bolt of lightning crashed into the forest. The car seemed to be stuck in the mud, so I jumped out to help try and free the car. Suddenly the whole world seemed to be lit up like a beacon. With an earsplitting crash at the same time a bolt of lightning had struck a tree, flinging me to the ground. As I pulled myself back to my feet, I could see by the lights of the car that a huge branch had fallen across the car, trapping those inside. I rushed over to try and rescue the trapped people, when a fresh flash of lightning lit the scene and my heart stopped.

There trapped in the driving seat was my Bekki! Blood trickled from her lips, and she tried to smile.

"Fancy meeting you here" she muttered

"Hush" I said "I will have you free in a moment"

She grabbed my hand, "Leave me" She tried to turn her head, to where I now saw a small frightened child sat strapped in the back seat.

"Save your daughter" she smiled.

My mouth dropped open, my daughter, what did she mean? A fresh crash of thunder brought me back to my senses. I was a Ranger, and I had a job to do. All my questions could be answered later.

I reached in and carefully lifted the frightened child from the car, leaning forward I kissed Bekki.

"It's alright love, I'll be back for you" I said sounding as confidant as I could.

I rushed to my car, placing the girl inside, before running back to my trapped Bekki.

"She is safe" I told her, but the smells of petrol from the crushed car made me think otherwise about Bekki and I.

I tried to lift the branch but it was too heavy.

"Go" said Bekki "It is no use, just remember I love you, and have always loved you"

No use! no use! My heart shouted, finding a daughter, finding I still had my love. I needed strength, now more than at any time before, I needed the green mist.

Grasping the branch with my hands, rain streaming down my face, I started to try and lift it. I cried out to the forest to give me strength. I thought of all that had gone before, the pain, the heartache, and the loneliness. I concentrated everything into the thought of the mist. Suddenly it was there, crashing through my mind, covering the noise of the storm as it filled my whole being.

I came to, lying on the ground, my head reeling and blood dripping from my hands. The branch was moved from the car. I tried to stand every part of my body screaming with the effort. I managed to drag the now unconscious Bekki from the car, eventually taking her to the safety of my own vehicle to join our daughter.

I did not know how, but something had changed, the green mist had come, and with the effort, almost like a goodbye had gone, and I knew in my heart it would never come back again.

I put the car into gear, and as I did the rest of the tree crashed down, crushing Bekki's car.

And so, we drove to the hospital, a new life ahead of us, thanks to the green mist.

Storyheart

SIX THOUSAND MILES

The silver line of a passing plane, like a snail's trail snaked across the blue sky, dodging around the puffball clouds. He looked up, shading his eyes as he watched the speck grow smaller until it disappeared into the setting sun.

His mind wandered back to his own flight, and to where he was now, the words that often spun through the cobwebs of his mind surfaced once more.

Six thousand miles, and seven hours, from all he'd ever known
Way, way across the silver sea, from what he still called home

He was that and more, all his history, all his memories were those many miles away. Sure the telephone and the emails brought people closer, but they could never replace the memories of his life up to now

He walked back into the house, his eyes automatically going to the array of faces that lined the cabinet top, each smiling picture a memory of a family he spoke to but did not see. He wondered how much the children had grown, what they were doing and missed them all once more.

It had not been something he had looked for that day, he had gone into a totally different chat room to the one he normally visited on the internet. He was a regular on the cyber highway and had many friends around the world. He would never know just what made him go into that chatroom that day, but he went and as normal started chatting to various people.

Then she was there, it started as the normal gentle banter between chatroom folk, but soon they began to realize that this was something different. They met the next

Stories from the Heart

night and the next night and the next. Gradually getting to know each other better, and learn about each other. They found that they could tell each other the most intimate things, things that they had bottled up deep inside them for many years. And with each revelation, they both began to realize that this was not just an online romance, it was something deeper, it was meant to be.

Days turned into weeks, weeks into months, until one day she let him phone her, and hearing her voice had sent bells ringing though his heart.

But life was not easy, it never is. Theirs was not a simple affair, a romance that could be reached easily. For one thing, a large ocean separated the two people, and for a second, neither of them was free to be with the other.

From early on, they had realized that things were not what they had seemed. Each of them knew of the other's problems and unhappiness.

Rather than remember the hurt and the pain of what happened next, his mind, like a scratched record, skipped over most of the details

Flashes of crying curled up in a ball, of breaking down at work, and letting his manager know about what was going on. The way people had taken sides, hurting everybody with their own petty spite, poison pen letters, even to crashing his home computer and capturing and editing emails. Friends were lost and all had been hurt in so many ways.

He shivered; it had been beyond anything anybody could ever realize. But all the time they had a goal, a star they were reaching for.

As time went by and things gradually fell into some sort of order, the next step was getting across the ocean to be with her

He, for once, found some help and luck with his work. He had managed to get a transfer to the western colonies

Then, came the day his heart cried every time he thought of it. The day he left all he had ever known, left his beloved England, his family, his past, left it all to start from scratch in a new country. Saying good bye to his family, tears streamed down faces, not wanting to leave. But at the same time his heart had told him, what he was doing was right, and if it was right then he should do it.

She had been there at the airport, falling into his arms, and both of them knew what they were doing despite all that had gone before, the hurt, the pain, and all that was yet to come. This was right, this was what was meant to be.

They started a life together, at first only managing short periods of time with each other while she had gone through the same hurt with her divorce as he had done with his. Still this time, she was not alone, he was there, and he tried every way he could to help her. It was not easy, it was a different country and everything was strange to him.

He remembered holding her sobbing through the night, with such a feeling of helplessness that his heart had thought it would break.

He looked up once more at the disappearing plane, and the silver trails left like a ghost writing in the sky

Six thousand miles, and seven hours, from all he'd ever known
Way, way across the silver sea, from what he still called home

His thoughts were interrupted by the sound of small footsteps climbing up the steps, and he looked down as a small hand reached for his, and a pair of eyes as blue as his own looked up at him filled with such love.

"Daddy, Daddy, up" said a small voice, and as he lifted his daughter into his arms, his wife with their newborn son came into the room.

"Missing home again?" she smiled at him, as it was more like a statement than a question

"No love" he smiled back, putting his arm around his wife so the four of them could hug together

"I am home."

Six thousand miles, and seven hours, from all he'd ever known
Way, way across the silver sea, from what he still called home
To follow ones heart, and reach the star, that which was meant to be
Six thousand miles and seven hours, to a love and his new family

Storyheart

THE RACE

His hands moved and opened the album in front of him, the story was his each page told how it had been.

He turned to the first entry..

Thursday December 28th
The post arrives and I receive a shock, what I thought was an impossible dream had become a reality, I've been accepted to run in "THE LONDON MARATHON"!!!.

What an error, here I am nearly 38 years of age, with a body that has seen better days. A person who hasn't done a lot of exercise except running around at work and the odd game of badminton, since two operations on my left knee two years ago. "WHAT HAVE I GONE AND LET MYSELF IN FOR!!!!!"

Wow!! What a shock that day had been. He remembered, he never thought he would have been lucky enough to get a place, but oh what a daunting thought when he found he had been lucky enough to be granted one.

He remembered the early days of his running, the jogs around the block, the aches and the pains, but as he read on, the days became more interesting and his training runs became longer.

Monday, January 8th-Sunday, January 14th
Monday: No badminton yet, so another trip around my 4.5 miles circuit. Ran reverse way round the course, complete with long hill, at least I got around.

Stories from the Heart

Tuesday: You get some funny looks as you pound the local streets and even the odd "hello" from other passing lunatic's, the old knee has started complaining about having to do so much work. Covered about 5 miles this evening, purchased another knee bandage.

Wednesday: Knee still aching, have taken the night off to rest the weary joints, thinking of buying shares in Boots, with all these bandages, I might end up running dressed up as an Egyptian Mummy.

Those had been hard days, running around the streets in all sorts of weather. As the days went on and the race came nearer, he had enjoyed them more and more. He had discovered parts of his body and parts of his neighborhood that he never knew existed before.

He flicked through the pages, reading about the miles he had traveled, and the odd joke he had still been able to make about the runs and things that had happened to him.

Then a week before the actual race was an entry that proved, at least, if nothing else, he had still managed to have a sense of humor.

Sunday, April 8th-Saturday, April 14th
The last full week of training, started with my losing a battle with a car and a horse for the right of way and ending up, yes, in another ditch. This left me 5 miles to run with one very wet and muddied leg and foot. This week saw a regular service along the old railway line, and another night when I got lost, ending up running round local point to point horserace course. Had a refusal at the open ditch fence and another muddied foot! I ran for a total of 40 miles this last week, one week to go, time to recover and get the body and soul ready for next weekend.

He turned over the page of the book, and found a number. He smiled remembering the actual day of the race and the feeling of wonder at all the tens of thousands of people that were there at the starting. Not knowing what the race would bring for him.

Storyheart

He remembered the thrill as the race started, being one of 30,000 runners, and all the training, the pain everything had been worthwhile for that moment on.

It must have been around 2 miles into 26 miles that he had found her, or rather found he was running at the same speed as the woman running beside him. A quick glance as they picked up their first water bottles had shown him a woman dressed much the same as him, with short dark hair and a body which would have at some other times have meant a lot to him. They carried on running together, smiling at each other at the comments from the massive crowd that lined the streets. Sharing the proffered sweets and oranges, while they learned about each other.

At around 10 miles, she stumbled on one of the thousand of discarded water bottles the lined the sides of the roads. Without thinking, he stopped and helped her to her feet, as his hand touched hers, and she looked up and smiled at him, the noise of the crowd seemed to roar in his ears, or was it his heart? They started to run again, somehow though their hands had still been joined as if it was the most natural thing to do. She turned and smiled at him "Thank you for that" she said "My name is Sarah." Again she smiled and his tired legs seemed to find new life as he introduced himself to her, and they chatted as they continued to run hand in hand.

Each stop after that, they shared the water bottle and shared the pain of the miles as they ran through the sights and the sounds of the London streets. Suddenly they crossed Tower Bridge for the 2nd time and he realized they had only 5 miles to go. Their talk became shorter as they both began to suffer these last miles. His leg cramped up, and she stopped and with hands that sent electric shocks through his heart gently massaged his calves until once more they started again. As they ran over the cobble stones of the Tower of London, their hands found each other's again.

They never let go during the last two miles of the race, gently squeezing each other's hand to give encouragement, until they turned at Buckingham Palace with just 200 yards to go.

They crossed the finishing line hands held high, still joined together, smiles as wide as the River Thames across their faces.

They collapsed into each other's arms, and for the first time, he tasted her lips as they kissed each other, a kiss that meant more to him than finishing the 26 miles. More than any medal ever could.

As they collected their foil blankets and chomped on the proffered food, they made an agreement to meet once they had reclaimed their clothes.

Shuffling as fast as his rapidly ceasing legs would let him, he'd fought his was through the masses of runners and greeters to collect his clothes and put them on before going in search of Sarah.

He looked for her, trying to keep moving, his muscles screaming at the effort. But it had been fruitless from the start, there was just too many people, to find one person in the tens of thousands all high on their completion of the marathon, and was just not possible.

He had wandered around for hours getting colder, feeling more and more lonely, until with a sigh he had headed for the railway station and home.

Through the next weeks of collecting sponsorship money, and recovering, he had thought of Sarah often, and wondered if they would ever meet again.

He stopped and picked up the photo of him and Sarah crossing the finishing line as it lay in his book. He remembered receiving the race photo's some months later, and how his heart had leapt at seeing her.

A pair of hands rested on his shoulders, and a pair of soft lips kissed his cheek.

"Ah, the photo" said a voice that still made his heart jump "The key to how we found each other"

He reached up and held the hand of his love. Both had the same idea, of tracking each other down from the race number clearly shown in the picture. Until three months after the day of the race they had once more held hands and kissed.

He closed the book that had been over a year ago, now they were again running with each other, still hand in hand, this time, in a bigger race. They were now a team, running the race of life together, forever.

(While nearly all of my stories are fictional, in this case I have used some my actual race log entries from my first ever London Marathon in 1990..Storyheart. Details of my London marathons can be found at http://4tenderheart.com/mara2k.html)

Stories from the Heart

LADY OF FASHION

It was in the early spring when I first noticed her. It was around the time that all the fashion houses were showing there spring collections. I had seen her before, our paths had crossed often. But this year, something was different, something drew me towards her.

She was dressed in a vivid green, looking fresh and new, vibrant and bright. She stole my heart in those early days. All was new and she taught me to see things I had never noticed before. My life was one of new beginnings and she was with me all the time.

Days turned into months and spring turned into summer.

As the sun shone on us, my love grew. She glowed in the brightness of our being together. Her clothes were now bright and brilliant, yellows, blues and greens, each day something worth seeing. Each day, I fell deeper under her spell. I did not realize just how deep I was falling under her spell. I was hers, and she was mine. Hazy shimmering days of warmth and love, being together though the long daylight hours and the short restful nights wrapped in the gentle breeze of summer and our love.

As the months changed, so did she, the brightness of her summer fashion gave way to reds and gold's. Still we were together. Though sometimes things got rough, I knew her love was there for all to see. Long walks, crunching leaves beneath my feet, with her arms around me, knowing happiness like I had never known before.

Time moved on and she chilled, her colors sometimes white against winter's nights. But all the while I knew such

Storyheart

a deep love, all the time, through every cold or angry moment, I still loved her.

And so a year rolled by. A year since I had first noticed her. A year, when through every change she had made to herself, I had known her love.

After all, this was my country, no matter what colors mother nature garbed her in. This was my home, and I loved her dearly.

(An Englishman will always think of England no matter where he goes..Storyheart)

ROMANCE

She sat thinking about her life, the problems that were going on, that seemed to be overwhelming her, work, love, all that she seemed to try went wrong. What else could she do, she did not really know which way to turn.

She stood up, suddenly feeling the need to get out of her small room, to get out of the box she felt closing in around her.

She drove to a small wooded area, on the edge of the town, she now called her home. Driving only half knowing where or why she drove. And when she turned off the car engine, she still did not know just why she was there, and exactly where she was.

She got out of the car, picked up a spare bottle of water she had left from her trip to work and started making her way down the path that lead into the wood.

As she moved through the trees the branches seemed to meet over her head like a green canopy, sun light dappled through the branches, spreading moving patterns of light around the world she now moved through. Ahead she could just make out a small clearing, it seemed almost like it was made for her. Quietly, scared to make a sound for fear of breaking the silence, she entered the glade. There she sat on a log and sipped her water.

It was so quiet, so peaceful, almost at once her restless mind started to calm, thoughts that had been tossed around like a small ship on an ocean, now started to form sense and reason.

She sat and thought about her life, as the sun set, and the red touch of evening filled the sky, a small noise near her brought her from her thoughts. She looked down and noticed several small rabbits that now played and ate near her, seemingly taking no notice of her. As she watched, a young deer slowly entered the glade from the woods edge. She sat still, not wanting the break the spell or frighten any of the animals. The evening felt the first hint of night's chill and the animals left the glade. Slowly she got up and found her way back to the car.

She drove back to the flat, her mind seemingly at peace.

From that day on, she often went back to the glade, each time putting her life back into some form of order. The animals seeming to know her and accept her. Through the spring she learned more about them and their ways.

Then one day, as she entered the glade, she noticed another person sitting on her log. She approached, not wanting to break the spell that the glade held. It was a man, about her own age, who seemed lost and trapped in the magic of the glade she knew so well.

She moved next to him, and he jumped, "Sorry" she said, "I did not mean to startle you."

And that was the start, they talked in soft whispers finding out about each other. As they sat, the animals came to meet their friend and her new man, that even now was starting to become part of her life.

Days turned into weeks, weeks into months, and the seasons came and went. Though they did meet and go out, the glade was still their special place, their refuge. As winter turned to spring and everything started to blossom and grow, so did their love. Then one day he asked her to marry him, there in the grove that had become a second home to them.

Six months later, beside the log where the animals still played in the autumn light, a wedding bouquet was left, as the two of them shared their marriage with the glade.

Years went by and the leaves turned through their full range of colors. And as with the seasons bringing forth new life, so did their marriage. The visitors to the glade went from two to three, to four. They lived their lives happy, as one with the world, a world forever blessed by the special spot, where they first met.

SILVER

The chill of the air turned each breath to a cloud as it left his mouth. The weak sun tried to push itself through the gray snow laden skies. He looked at his compass, and once more pushed onwards, quickly gazing at the ever threatening clouds. His feet crunched the fresh snow underfoot, snow that he knew any moment would be joined by much more from the ever darkening sky.

He knew to be caught out in the woods in the soon to hit blizzard would be fatal. He had to reach the cabin; he knew was just a few miles away.

Brushing through the fir trees, he suddenly came to a clearing in the forest, and there in the middle was a huge wolf. He stopped, not knowing what to do. The wolf looked up, and a pair of huge brown eyes seemed to pierce his very soul.

It was at that moment the skies opened, and the blizzard hit, blowing away vision and instantly turning the world into a white hell. The wind whipped the snowflakes, making any exposed skin feel like a thousand needles had pricked it. He pulled the hood of his jacket tighter around his face, trying to look at the compass once more. Then putting his head down he set out once more, struggling every step against the bitter wind and driving snow. His vision was useless, he could see but a few inches in front of him.

He lost all sense of time and direction. His fingers fumbled for the compass, but frozen with cold, lost his grip and it fell into the fresh snow. He blindly pushed on each step an effort one foot in front of the other he struggled onwards. He did not know how many times he had fallen, but each time he pushed himself back to his feet and struggled onward. His mind must be playing tricks, but he was sure he could make out a pale light moving amongst the trees. He tried to make an effort to move towards it, but his feet would not move and he fell once more into the snow. He attempted to get up, but his head swam with the effort. Darkness covered him and he felt no more. His eyes flicked open once and he saw the light getting closer. He vainly tried to cry out before the darkness covered him again. Just as the edges of his vision disappeared he thought that he saw two brown pools of fire looking at him.

He woke up to feel the warmth spreading through his body. A soft light of a flickering log fire cast shadows across the ceiling. He felt the soft warmth of fur across his body, and another body stirred next to his. An arm wrapping around him before the darkness once more covered him.

Slowly, his eyes cleared and he found himself looking into a face of surely what must be an angel. A smile that would alone have removed the cold of any blizzard, and a pair of brown eyes that were vaguely familiar made him feel that indeed he had died and gone to heaven.

He tried to sit up and the room swam before his eyes. "Shhhhhhhh now," a soft voice said. "Take it easy you have had a rough time." This time he tried to move more slowly and he managed to get himself into a sitting position. When he looked up, she had disappeared. He looked around, so he had made it to the cabin after all.

The sound of pans being moved was soon followed by the smell of food being cooked. And suddenly he felt really hungry. She appeared with a plate of food and a mug of steaming coffee. They started to talk as the food filled the emptiness of his stomach. Her name, she told him, was Sheriva, which she said was silver in her native tongue. She dipped her head and he saw the strands of silver hair that made a streak amongst the rest of the black raven locks, and he knew why.

Storyheart

She had been out in the forest herself, but had reached the cabin before the blizzard broke. She told him how some sense had made her go looking but did not go into it any more than that. They talked as the blizzard hammered at the cabin. The fire dwindled and they talked on, until the last flames disappeared. His eyes started to close and he felt her slip under the covers, her body warm beside his. The moon's silver beam filtered through the snow covered windows, as their bodies found each other, like a halo of silver it surrounded their love making. They were safe inside the walls of the cabin, wrapped safe within each other's arms.

As he slowly came awake, he felt the warmth of her body next to his and the softness of the fur. The fur!! He moved away fast, looking at a large wolf that was lying next to him. He shivered, he had heard of these mountain tales, of wolves that mysteriously turned into women in the light of the moon. Remembering what had gone before, he shivered again. A soft laugh floated across the cabin. So, you have met my friend she said. The day passed as the blizzard continued to howl outside. He got used to the presence of the wolf, which he found actually gave him some peace of mind. They talked, they kissed, and they loved. He told her all about himself, his dreams, his fears, his happiness, and his sadness. Without saying a word, she listened and answers came into his head. When he cried, she held him, when he laughed she laughed with him. As the moon once more filled the sky, she let the wolf out and slowly closed the door.

"The storm is almost over. It will be clear by tomorrow," she said. "I wish that it would never end," he replied. Knowing in his heart that this was indeed what he wanted. "Do you?" she asked with a questioning look. "Yes," he replied, more sure than ever before. "We will see," she softly said.

They made love that night, reaching higher and higher into the stars. Until the first tip of the sun's rays pierced the sky, they came together, in what could only be called a howl of ecstasy.

He fell asleep, and dreamed of running through the forest. He woke to feel the fur next to him, so the wolf was back. He opened his eyes, stroking the body next to him. As he looked he noticed a silver streak of fur, down the wolf's back. And as he stirred the wolf shimmered, turning into the shape of Sheriva. He found that he was not amazed at this, as if he already knew. She smiled at him.

"Come, Love, come run with me, be my mate, let us run these hills forever." She held out her hand, he grasped it. "Yes," he said, "forever". He felt his body change, suddenly he could smell the forest, could feel the earth. He looked across at his silver streaked mate. "Let us run together." Her voice spoke in his head. "Yes, Love," he replied. As they left the cabin and bounded into the fresh snow, many voices filled his head, welcoming him into the pack, mate of Sheriva.

Later that day, a rescue party made it to the cabin, but could find no trace of the man that they knew had been there.

Nobody noticed the two wolves that watched them from the edge of the woods.

MILLENIUM

The grey mist rolled across the marshes causing strange shapes to appear and disappear as if by magic. The scene was timeless and could have been from 10, 100 or even 1000 years ago. But it was now, the end of a millennium, the start of a new century.

A small light pierced the gloom, and if you looked deep at it you could see it was coming from a small window in an equally small and isolated cottage.

In the distance a clock from the church in the small village struck 9.

People all over the world were celebrating or getting ready to celebrate the new century. Huge parties were being planned or taking place even now, be it on a national or a small local scale. Where ever, everybody was set to enjoy this night.

That is everybody except me, if you looked into the window where the light shone, you would see me. I was there sitting at the table in the small cottage that I had rented.

I had chosen it to get as far away from the celebrations as I could. I sipped my tea, nothing stronger tonight, for the same reason as renting the cottage. I wanted to be on my own, after all what was there to celebrate?

My mind flicked back like a film on rewind, until as I flinched with the pain, it stopped and started to roll forward again. Then, in still photographs, scenes from the last year appeared.

A family laughing, loudly, the face of a beautiful, smiling woman, and two small angels.

A tear ran down my cheek and mingled with the others on the tabletop. The tea turned from warm to cold and the pictures in my mind changed. The 3 women in my life waving to me as they set off on a trip to their friends house, it was for a party, and my angels looked beautiful in their new party frocks. It was only 10 miles away, a 20-minute drive, not far at all.

After that, the pictures got confused, blurred. The knock at the door, the policeman and woman, telling me there had been an accident. The trip to the hospital, holding my wife's hand, and seeing the life drain from her eyes.

Not being allowed to see what was left of my angels after the firemen got them from the wrecked car. That is, until I had to identify what was left of them later.

Another tear splashed onto the table, they were really angels now. The funeral, vague faces, I could not remember anything, the photographs were so blurred, as was indeed, everything after that.

The empty house, the empty life.

Days came and went Christmas was nearly the end of me. I twice almost joined my loved ones, but each time something stayed my hand from taking those tablets I had bought for just that purpose. I could not go through the same again, so I had found a place I could hide away, forget the Millennium, the New Year, and forget life itself.

I sipped my tea, it was stone cold. The clock struck ten, and I moved to make a fresh cup. I was brought out of my thoughts by a small knocking on the door. At first, I did not move, but the knock came again. I drank the last drops of the cold tea, and dragged myself to the door. I opened the door, and at first, I couldn't see anybody. Then I looked down and a small face looked up at me.

I must have looked very rough, very wild. For as I looked at the small child, for that is what she was, she stepped back, and I thought she was going to run. She looked back at the gate, where I could see the shadowy figure of an adult.

The girl seemed to gain courage, and biting her lip, turned back to me, and pulling herself together, she started to repeat what she had obviously practiced. "My mummy and I wondered, as you are all alone, would you join

us to see in the Millennium?" she gasped at the end, and grinned an impish grin at the fact she had managed to get the words right. Her grin turned to a frown as I did not answer, and she looked back towards the gate. I could not answer, for the lump in my throat and I did not see the figure coming down the path.

I looked up as a quiet voice said "Lynn and I would be happy if you shared the New Year with us. We are just down the road, and like you, we too are alone." The tear veil cleared from my eyes and I looked into a pair of hazel eyes, where I saw a look of pleading cover one of despair that I knew so well. I did not know what to say, but when a small hand slipped into mine, I found myself soon being lead down the road with two strangers.

As the midnight hour came, I found a new century and a new beginning. The door for the future lay before me, and in the touch of a small hand and a pair of hazel eyes, my future and a new life was just beginning.

Stories from the Heart

CHRISTMAS STORY 1

She looked once again out of the window, surely it would snow, and it had to snow! It would not be Christmas without snow. Her Mother had told her earlier that day that there were snow clouds over head. But still there was no snow. She turned from the window, and looked at the room. Christmas decorations were in place, but somehow there was no sparkle, no Christmas spirit, it was as if the whole room was sad. As sad as her Mother she thought.

At that moment her Mother came in the room, she tried to raise a smile to her daughter, but the sadness behind her eyes showed through instead.

"Still no snow Rachel?" she said, trying hard to smile.

Something she had not been able to do since that day 6 months ago, when she had received a letter saying her husband had been lost while exploring some small backwater of the Amazon or some such place. He was always off somewhere or other on his geographical surveys. But that had been the last she had heard, all these months now here was Christmas, and it was just her and her daughter.

"No Mummy." replied her daughter, wanting to cry out at the sadness, and hurt she sensed in her Mother's voice. Though Rachel was only 7, she had tried so hard to make this Christmas better, but she could never make up for the sadness of being just the two of them.

"Rachel dear" said her Mother "Can you go down to the store, and try and get some holly so we can decorate the front door?"

Rachel gave her Mother a hug and put on her coat and headed for the store. She looked again at the skies, "Please let it snow" she whispered,

"Anything to make this Christmas special."

She entered the store, it was like entering another world, a fairy tale world of Christmas. The whole place was full of sparkling lights and glittering tinsel. Happiness filled the air. She sighed, thinking of the sadness in her own home. A smiling face topped by a red Christmas style hat greeted her. It was Mr Reggus, the owner of the store.

Rachel thought he must be related to Santa himself, so much did his smiling red face and bushy white beard, reminded her of dear old Santa.

"Well little Lady," he always called her little Lady "What can I do for you?"

She smiled, Mr Reggus always made her smile.

"Mr Reggus, my mother would like some holly to decorate our front door please." She always tried to be polite.

Mr Reggus smiled "Certainly little Lady."

He went to the back of the shop, and soon came back with several sprigs of holly, which he carefully wrapped in paper, so she would not hurt herself. As he went to hand her the parcel, he stopped. "Hmmm you've got the holly, but what about the mistletoe?" Rachel gave Mr Reggus a quizzical look.

"What is mistletoe?" she asked.

Mr. Reggus laughed, and told her all about the special power of Mistletoe and how there was magic in it that opened to anybody who kissed underneath it. He winked and produced a sprig, which he added to the parcel of holly.

She ran back to her waiting mother, she looked up as she went into the home, still no snow.

Her mother took the package of Holly and started to make her decorations for the door. Suddenly she started, coming across the mistletoe.

"What is this?" she asked her daughter.

"Mr. Reggus gave it to me." her daughter replied "He said it was Christmas magic."

Her mother turned away not wanting her daughter to see the tears in her eyes, if only she thought and let go a little sob. Her daughter went on, "Please Mummy, Mr. Reggus said we had to hang it above the door."

Her mother tried to smile and wiped away the tears. "Of course dear, we will put it above the door right now". She lifted her daughter and helped her pin the mistletoe above the door, then she kissed her daughter under it.

"There, sweetheart, a magical Christmas to you."

The rest of the day seemed to fly by and soon it was time for her to go to bed.

Christmas morn dawned and she woke to find a Christmas stocking on her bed, full of toys and goodies. She rushed into her mother's room to show her what Santa had left her, but her Mother was not there, the bed was crumpled, but she was not there.

Rachel went back to her room, got dressed and went downstairs, the lights were on and under the Christmas tree were a whole heap of presents. She wanted to open them, but was too worried about her Mother. It was Christmas, and she should be here to share it with her. She opened the door, and there under the mistletoe was her Mother, but not just her Mother, there was a stranger, a man, and he was kissing her mother. She stopped and her Mother turned, hearing her daughter behind her. A smile lit her face, something Rachel had not seen for a long time.

"Rachel darling," she held out her hand "come here, there is somebody I want you to meet." She took her daughter to a smiling man who only moments before had been kissing her Mother.

"Rachel, darling" smiled her Mother "This is your father, he has come home." She sobbed this time in happiness.

Rachel's eyes lit up as she recognized the man, it really was her father, he had come home, gently he picked her up hugging her to him, and as he did so, soft showers of snow

Storyheart

fell from his hair onto her face. These melted with the tears of happiness that fell from Rachel's eyes.

And so as in all good stories, it has come to a happy ending. Proving that the magic of Christmas really can happen.

Stories from the Heart

CHRISTMAS STORY 2

The dinner plates had been washed by an array of sometimes willing helpers, soft snores and full stomachs meant it was rest time before the evening present giving and more food. Children had been bribed with promises of things to come and were sleeping, or trying to sleep. A young girl sat resting her head on the legs of her sleeping Grandfather. Too excited to sleep, filled with the joys of Christmas, eyes as bright as the lights that twinkled on the tree.

The Grandfather opened his eyes and gave the girl a wink, "You ok love?" he whispered She smiled at the old man, "Yes, Grandfather" she said "I just can't seem to rest".

The old man patted his lap, "Come here sweetheart and I'll tell you a story".

Quickly, she climbed onto her Grandfather's lap and nestled into the old man's warm arms. She smiled up at him, "Grandfather, tell me a story of a Christmas when you were a boy".

A slow smile spread across the old man's face, followed by a flash of pain that filled his eyes with tears for a brief moment. The child did not see the look, she just snuggled down further, ready to listen to the old mans story.

I must have been just around eight, not much older than you. It was a Christmas like you see on Christmas cards, snow was all around, and that year people seemed to be more full of the Christmas spirit than normal. I had been looking forward so much to Christmas. Every day I had rushed home from school and down to the toyshop at

Storyheart

the end of the street. There, in the front window, was a magnificent toy fort full of shiny soldiers.

Each day I pressed my face against the window, checking that it was still there, until I knew every soldier, as if they were my own personal friends. I had dragged my parents to the shop any chance I could, making it no secret just what I wanted for Christmas this year. Each time I got the "Just wait and see." But I couldn't wait, each day I went and checked that the fort was still there, and each day it was. As Christmas grew nearer, I noticed a look of worry on my parents faces. I did not really understand what was going on. I heard talk of wars and battles, and soldiers seemed to fill the streets. But the only ones I was interested in were in the shop window.

Then one day I ran as normal to the toyshop, but the window was empty, the fort was gone. I ran home with tears streaming down my face, why had this happened? What had I done wrong? I ran sobbing into the house. My Mother came rushing out of the kitchen when she heard me, hands covered with flour from the cake baking. She hugged me to her as I told her between sobs of the disappearance of the fort. She hugged me again and she began to smile.

I looked past her, and for the first time caught site of my Father. He was dressed in Khaki, a uniform, as a soldier. I did not understand, and he hugged me to him, and tried to explain he had to go away for a while. He laughed and told me he would be back in a week or two. But the look on my Mother's face made me for a moment think something different. Before she too came and hugged me, her face full of smiles.

Two days later my Father went away, before he left he took me to one side.

"Son" he said "I have had a word with Santa Claus, and I think your Christmas will be just fine".

The next days leading up to Christmas I could hardly sleep. Then Christmas Eve came and I did not want to miss a thing, and I could not sleep just as you my

Granddaughter. My Mother came and read to me a letter from my Father, and hugged me until my eyes closed and I slept. I woke up the next morning and there it was at the foot of my bed, the fort, with all the soldiers I knew so well, looking even better than it had done in the shop.

Then Grandfather looked down, at the now sleeping girl on his lap. He sighed; glad he did not have to go on with the story. How would a young child like he had been understand about a black bordered telegram he had found his sobbing Mother holding, when he went to tell her about his present. I could not explain to her what it felt like to know his Father would not be coming home.

The fort had remained untouched and un-played with in his room, until his Mother finally gave it to a friend. He had cried for a week, and that Christmas never happened as far as he was concerned.

He looked again at his sleeping Granddaughter, and gave her a hug. Thank goodness such a thing would never happen again in her lifetime he thought.

She stirred and looked up at him with half closed eyes. "I love you Grandfather" she said.

And an old man cried.

Storyheart

CHRISTMAS STORY 3

Driving to work on a Sunday morning, the roads were fairly empty at the time of day I started work. Christmas lights still sparkled in the early morning light as I passed by the houses, reminding me it was only 3 days until Christmas. This was my first day back at work after several days off, and with so little time before Christmas, most people would now be on holiday for the next few days.

When I arrived at work, major problems were waiting for me and those few members of my shift not on vacation. The morning went by with many conference calls and problem resolving and around lunchtime, finally, I thought it had all settled down to a quieter day.

Suddenly my phone rang, it was my wife. The baby was sick, she had been crying for the last hour, and in pain. Not only that but when the baby had been sick she had traces of blood in the throw-up. She had phoned the doctor who had thought it was because of a cold and congestion. Naturally I was worried, our daughter was only seven months old after all, and so very precious to us.

I was getting on with more work, thinking about what was going on, when the phone went again. The Doctor had had second thoughts and wanted us to take the baby to the hospital. I would meet the rest of the family there.

I drove not quite knowing where I was going or what I was doing, the area was strange and the worry about what was going on weighing heavy on my mind.

I found the children's emergency area, I had arrived before my family. Soon we were all there. The baby was no her normal herself at all, she would not let you put her down, and was crying in pain, as well as constantly dribbling. We were quickly looked at and details taken, and then started a long wait until we could be seen. Children and families came and went and still we waited. Our other children were starting to get fractious, we had by this time been waiting almost three hours.

At last we were called in, and shown to the smallest cubical out of the ones there were, this was for the two of us, the baby, two small children and all the bags and car seats that were needed to transport the family around. The staff seeing that the children with nothing to do, brought them gifts from the hospital Christmas tree, and so we waited.

Another hour, and at last the doctor came to see us. The baby was checked out, and nothing could be found. People still came and went and time continued to pass. At last the doctor came back and advised that they were going to take x-rays of the baby. We talked about what to do, we had been at the hospital for over 4 hours, the children were tired and hungry, and we both knew how long x-rays could take. Neither of us wanted to leave, but though it best if my wife took the children home and I stayed.

Very quickly we went to the x-ray area, and after just ten minutes were back with the films. The doctor could see nothing on the x-rays, but wanted a second opinion. The Senior Doctor came and examined the baby, and suddenly reported to both myself and the other doctor that she could see something trapped at the back of the baby's throat. This explained her pain, and the soaking shoulders I now had from her constant dribbling for the last several hours I had held her.

My heart jumped into my throat, what had she swallowed, what if it moved and lodged across her throat. The surgeon was paged, and I was taken with the baby into another area. I tried to keep her as quiet as possible, the Christmas angels pinned round the walls seemed to look down at her so small in my arms and in so much pain. We moved to behind a curtain, as a major case was coming in, all the time the doctors kept checking on us. Nurses peered in at the beautiful baby, who every now and then let out such a heart rending cry that all stopped to see what was wrong.

The surgeon came and explained what he had to do, it was thought better to operate on the baby to get rid of the obstruction, rather than cause her even more distress, and possible problems by fishing for it while she was awake. The operating room was ready; we went up and met the operating team, where I handed over my beloved daughter to them. I waited in and empty waiting area.

Christmas lights sparkled on windows, and season's decorations were everywhere. I phoned my now tearful wife, and explained what was going on. Thoughts went to another baby all those years ago, and silent prayers were sent to him. The last words that the anesthetist had said to me as she took the baby, swirled around my head again, and again.

"You are very lucky, 80% of babies who swallow things like this do not even make it to the hospital"

What would we do if anything happened to her? After all that had happened to us this last year, this would be the end of all and everything if we lost her.

After what seemed an age, but was actually only 20 minutes the doctor returned, holding in his hand a container in which was a small frog foil sticker, as used on cards and presents at Christmas. This was the offending object. The baby was ok, and was waiting for me in the recovery area.

I sat by her bed, waiting for her to recover, trying to smile at the comments of the nurse taking care of her. She was alright, she was safe, a small tear trickled down my face, and my heart smiled at the beauty that was our daughter now safe and sound sleeping soundly next to me.

A half hour later she was awake, and her smiling self, drinking a bottle of juice as if nothing had happened. Once we had been checked out, we left for our drive back home. The Christmas lights now matching the pair of sparkling eyes that sat in the car seat next to me.

We arrived home in the early hours of the morning, safe and sound, but still the words echoed around my mind. 80% of babies never make it to the hospital.

As we hugged each other and the baby, we both realized the Christmas gift we had just been given. Never mind that Christmas was still two days away. We had already received the greatest Christmas present we would ever have. The safety and well being of our baby.

Storyheart

CHRISTMAS STORY 4

She stood in the street, soft snowflakes falling around her, as she gazed at the doll in the shop window. The bright lights of Christmas filled the night, casting shadows of all shapes and sizes across the white winter blanket that covered the streets. Sounds of music and laughter came from behind curtains, and the spirit of the Yuletide seemed to fill the air.

Children their faces lit with the joy of the season rushed through the streets, their multicolor garb making her drab dress look even duller.

She looked once more at the doll in the window a look of longing covered her face, as she wiped away a small teardrop that escaped the corner of one eye.

The shop door opened as a family, arms filled with gifts came laughing into the street, and without thinking she slipped past them into the shop. Her eyes opened wide as she gazed on the beauties in this Aladdin's cave of a toyshop. Not knowing where to look first she slowly wondered through the store, each step revealing something even more fantastic, even more wonderful. Her eyes grew as big as saucers, and sparkled like the lights that lit the Christmas bedecked store.

At last she came to the dolls, and she knew at once the one she wanted, the one she had craved for such a long. She was there, her dark hair curled around her face, blue eyes smiled at the girl, and hands were outstretched as if asking to be taken and held by the girl.

Tears sprang to the young girl's eyes, slowly trickling down her cheek, as she knew she would never have the doll, never know the feel of her cuddled up in her arms.

Slowly she turned and walked back through the store. Nobody seemed to notice the girl, in her dull dress, with her tear smeared features and a heart so heavy one could almost feel the pain.

She reached the door as another family came rushing into the store, and for a moment the girl wanted to stay and join them, then as before she quietly moved through the door, until she stood once more on the street gazing at the doll in the shop window.

It was the same place she had been standing all those years ago, when the runaway coach and horses had plowed into her, sending her to the world where she now roamed.

With a sigh that if heard would have broken your heart, she reached towards the doll, her ghostly hands passing through the window, and also through the doll. With tears still falling from her deep rimmed eyes she turned and walked away disappearing into the growing darkness. She would be back next year, once more to see the doll and each year after that until she would finally rest in peace.

About the Author

Storyheart (Barry Eva) was born in Barnet, Hertfordshire, England in 1952. He sang and performed from an early age, writing songs and poems, before moving onto children's stories, some of which were performed as musicals. In 1998 he wrote his first Love Story, and has not stopped writing them since.

Thousands have read and enjoyed his stories on the Internet, now he is sharing them with a wider audience.

He paints pictures of life and love many can relate to, all being written from the heart.

In 2000, he left his beloved England and following his heart, moved to the USA, where he lives with his new family.